"DID YOU F

Sammi lowered her gaze and noticed Nick was gripping the edge of the table so hard his knuckles were white. She glanced back at his face. He was turned sideways in his chair, his body facing her but his head was turned away again. That muscle in his jaw ticked once, twice.

This was it, then. The moment of truth. "No," she told him, "I didn't forget."

He whipped his head around, shock plain on his face.

With her heart pounding clear up into her throat, Sammi tried to swallow. It didn't work. She glanced away from him. "That is, unless you've . . . changed your mind."

"Not on your life, lady," Nick said softly. "As long as you really mean it."

Sammi felt a sharp new fear. Before this night was over, she and Nick were going to make love. She knew it, wanted it. Every cell in her body begged for it. But . . . what if she failed to please him?

JANIS REAMS HUDSON

Sammi's Heart

ZEBRA BOOKS
KENSINGTON PUBLISHING CORP.

ZEBRA BOOKS

are published by

Kensington Publishing Corp.
475 Park Avenue South
New York, NY 10016

First printing: September, 1992

Printed in the United States of America

This book is dedicated in loving memory to Claude O. Reams, my father, for instilling in me a love of planes and flying. In particular, flying by the seat of my pants. He also showed me the value and thrill of occasionally breaking the rules and beating the odds. During recent years, he taught by example what courage, stubbornness, strength of will, and an unconquerable sense of humor can accomplish.

Thank you, Daddy. I miss you. As you said, it is good to hold on to the memories.

ACKNOWLEDGMENTS

Without the generosity, enthusiasm, and patience of the people at Gulfstream Aerospace Technologies in Oklahoma City, this book would not have been possible. Several of them deserve special thanks for putting up with me and my questions:

Wayne Radko, Controller
"Savannah" Joe Frederick, Director, Manufacturing Engineering
Cliff Shirley, Director, Commander Programs
Donna Boyd, Senior Secretary, Operations
Sue McGlynn, Executive Secretary, Administration
Chick Tonelis, Aircraft Mechanic, Retired

Thanks, too, to the ladies on the Video Jet Paint Marker, for letting me watch them work, and to Karren Radko, President of Oklahoma Romance Writers of America, for opening the doors of Gulfstream to me and setting up my tour.

Additional thanks go to Dotty Cheek, National Business Aircraft Association; Kaaran Anderson, Public Relations, Palmer House, Chicago; Dave Riley, Toys for Big Boys, Oklahoma City; and John Klingstedt, world traveler and generous friend.

Two books I found helpful were *Careers in Aviation* by Sharon Carter (Rosen Publishing Group, Inc., NY, 1990) and *Opportunities in Aerospace Careers* by Wallace R. Maples (VGM/NTC Publishing Group, 1991).

Thanks, too, to my brother, Ron Reams, for his invaluable information, insight, and hand-holding. Long live the Belchfire!

One

Dozens of floral arrangements decorated every available surface of the private room in Oklahoma City's Baptist Medical Center, but they weren't cheering the patient.

"I thought you were more than just an employee," Henry said with a pout. "I thought during the past couple of years you and I had become friends."

Sammi Carmichael bit back a grin. "Henry—"

"A friend would tell me what's going on at the plant."

"Nice try," Sammi said. "You're flat on your back in the hospital, you've just suffered a heart attack—"

"A mild one."

"And you say you're retiring—"

"I have retired."

"Have retired, then. What good will talking about the plant do except get me thrown out of here by your doctors?"

"Come on, Sammi. Nick's coming in today to

take over. He's going to ask questions. I can't tell my own son I don't know what the devil's going on at my own company, can I?"

"Henry, Henry." Sammi shook her head in mock dismay. Privately she was amazed at the ease with which Henry spoke Nick's name. To hear Henry tell it, he and his son did nothing but argue whenever they got within shouting distance of each other.

Sammi had experienced for herself that Henry spoke the truth. She had been around only one time when the two men were together. That incident a couple of years ago, the first time she had talked to Henry about one of her ideas for the company, had been enough for her. Henry had gone beyond rudeness. Not with her, but with his son. The mere memory of the confrontation between Henry and Nick Elliott made her uncomfortable.

Henry was like two different men. Sharp, friendly, and outgoing to all who knew him, but with Nick he became sarcastic, argumentative, and *very* unpleasant. Henry got angry just talking about Nick.

But now, while recovering from a heart attack, was not the time for Henry to get worked up about his son. Sammi decided to distract him.

"Actually," she said, "I think this was all a ploy on your part. Boot me up out of production onto Mahogany Row with a nice, cushy desk job, then leave me to sink or swim on my own."

Henry chuckled. "You've had the job barely two weeks. You can't be sinking yet. I thought we agreed a long time ago those self-doubts of yours were groundless. Besides. You're the strongest swimmer I know."

Sammi smiled. "What self-doubts?" The majority of her old insecurities were long gone. Those that hadn't been laid to rest with Jim had surely been burned to cinders ages ago in the fire of enthusiasm she felt for her job at Elliott Air. No more lack of confidence for her. Only a tiny insecurity here and there. Nothing to worry about. Sometimes, though, the memories of pain and uncertainty haunted her.

"I see that look in your eyes," Henry said. "You still remember feeling like a mouse. You're no mouse, Sammi. You never were."

"Oh yes I was, and you know it. I'll never forget how scared I was that first time I talked to you."

"So you were nervous." Henry waved his hand as if shooing away the idea of her fear. "You didn't let it stop you. You were stronger than you thought. How else do you explain the way you confronted me by the coffee machine that day in the plant? I know my reputation as well as you do. What you said to me then took guts."

She gave a slight shrug. "I didn't say much."

"No, only that we were throwing enough material into the Dumpster each week to build entire airplanes. You got my attention, too."

Sammi smiled. "Yeah, I guess I did, didn't I?"

"And you were right. You know how right you were. You get a percentage of the amount the company saves in your paycheck every month because of that computer program you recommended that tells us how to cut our materials. These days we don't waste enough material to sneeze at. Then there's the new clamp you came up with, and the inventory control system you recommended."

"Why are we talking about this?" Sammi asked. "It's old news."

"I'm just reminding you how valuable you are to the company. If I didn't think—know—you had what it takes to do your new job, I never would have promoted you."

Sammi looked down and wound her purse strap around her index finger. "I know that."

"Do you?"

She glanced up and saw him watching her through narrowed eyes. She straightened her shoulders and let go of her purse. "Yes. I do."

Henry studied her a full minute longer, then nodded. "Good. Because Nick's not going to cut you or anyone else any slack at the plant. He's tough and he's fair, but he's not the type—" Henry grimaced, then grinned. "Let's just say Nick's not as nice a guy as I am. You're going to have to prove yourself to him."

Sammi gave Henry a wry grin. "I'll do my best."

"You just keep your chin up. You'll do fine."

"I will. Now, can we talk about something else? Something more pleasant, like when they plan to let you go home?"

Henry grinned. "According to my doctor, if I'm a good boy I can go home tomorrow."

Sammi laughed and took his hand. "You've never been a good boy."

"Well, don't tell my doctor."

"When do you expect Nick to get here?"

"Nick's here."

At the sound of a third voice in the room, Sammi jerked to let go of Henry's hand. He held on. He tried to tell her something with his eyes, but she couldn't read the message. She tugged again to free herself, and again, he kept his hold.

Finally Henry turned his head toward the door. So did Sammi.

Nick Elliott stood in the doorway. Tall and lean, he commanded attention by his very presence. She saw the breadth of his shoulders, his shocking blue eyes, icelike in their coldness, his dark brown hair, his firm, well-shaped mouth. He exuded raw masculine intensity. Something deep inside Sammi's chest fluttered.

Then he looked her in the eye and the most frightening thing happened. Those walls of self-assurance she had built up over the past three years wobbled.

Sammi tensed. She wasn't sure how she knew, or how he might go about it, but clear down in her bones she was certain this man could destroy her. Shaken, she glanced at Henry for reassurance.

Henry seemed to be having his own problems. The emotions that crossed his face while he looked at his son worried her. Pain, anger, resignation. They flashed through his eyes distinctly, one at a time, before he managed to control his expression.

"Nick," he said.

13

Nick came forward, bold determination in every step. "Henry."

Sammi read the speculation in Nick's eyes. A young woman sitting beside his father's hospital bed, holding the man's hand . . . Nick obviously was not thinking what good, platonic friends she and Henry must be. Why wouldn't Henry let go? Did he want his son to get the wrong impression?

"Glad you're here," Henry said to Nick.

Nick slid his hands into his pockets and stepped closer to the bed. "A simple retirement would have done it. The heart attack was hardly necessary."

The coldness in his voice made Sammi shiver. What was it with these two men? What was it with *this* man, that he could generate in her both feminine interest . . . and fear?

"Hmmph," Henry said. "With you, I never know."

As if finally remembering her presence, Henry added, "I don't think the two of you have been properly introduced. Samantha Carmichael works for us. Sammi, my son, Nick."

Nick's eyes widened fractionally.

Sammi schooled her features to hide her sudden nervousness. Henry called it her ice maiden look. Jim had said worse. Much worse. But then, Jim had always been free with his criticism of her. She couldn't help it if the fear and insecurities she felt inside appeared on her face as coolness, aloofness. It was her mask of protection. A familiar crutch she'd never known she used until Henry had made her see it. She hadn't felt the need for that old

14

crutch in ages. Not until Nick Elliott looked her in the eye.

She watched him now, trying to see even a tiny part of Henry's open friendliness in him. It wasn't there. Nick's blue eyes were shaped like Henry's gray ones, but where Henry's twinkled, Nick's shot fiery hostility. Their mouths might be similar, but Henry's smiled while Nick's frowned. Two faces physically similar, with two personalities that were polar opposites.

Sammi took a deep breath and made herself nod at Nick. "Nice to see you again." *I think.*

At Nick's questioning look, Henry said, "You met her a couple of years ago. Sammi's the one who talked me into getting that nester system that tells us how to cut our sheet metal."

Nick's eyes narrowed. Sammi could tell the minute he remembered the afternoon in question, the terrible argument he and his father had that day, the horrible way Henry had treated him. Given a choice, Sammi would have chosen to be left out of that memory. Nick's hostile gaze told her he not only recalled her part in the scene but also resented her for it.

"That was just the first of Sammi's good ideas," Henry said.

Nick looked at his father, at Henry and Sammi's joined hands, then back at Sammi. His expression changed to wry amusement. "I'll bet."

Assertive. That's what people at work called her. Where was that assertiveness now? She shouldn't let Nick's attitude rattle her. But it did. She tugged

15

on her hand once more, and this time Henry let her go.

"Yes." By the look on Henry's face, he was purposely ignoring the undercurrents in the room. "In fact, our Sammi's come up with so many good ideas I decided her talents were being wasted in production."

Nick's hard blue eyes gave her the once-over. "I can see why you wouldn't want our Sammi's talents to be wasted."

It took all Sammi's strength to keep from cringing—or sneering right back at him, she didn't know which. She straightened her shoulders. "Henry—"

"Booted her upstairs just a couple of weeks ago," Henry interrupted. "Sammi's now Director of Advanced Technology."

The raised eyebrow Nick turned on his father said he knew full well there had never been any such position or department at Elliott Air. "How many people do we have in, what is it? Advanced Technology?" Nick asked.

Sammi felt herself blush, and was furious with herself for it. There was no need to get embarrassed or defensive. She should be used to reactions like Nick's by now. Lord knew, every staff member at Elliott Air had raised a brow when Henry had promoted her. Yet after a mere two weeks, they seemed to have accepted her. As much as they could accept any woman in what they considered all-male territory.

Henry grinned at Nick. "How many people? Just one."

Nick gave Sammi a slow, angled nod. "Good for you." Then he turned back to Henry. "Any other *surprises* waiting for me?"

Sammi ground her teeth. Oh, she knew exactly what he was thinking, what Henry was letting him think, leading him to think. And she intended to set Nick straight. But now was not the time. Not in Henry's hospital room.

When Henry launched into details about production quotas and deadlines, Sammi picked up her purse. Nick Elliott made her nervous. She wanted out of there. She waited for a break in Henry's monologue, then said, "I'll go so you two can talk."

When she stood, Henry held a hand out to her. She took it and gave him a smile, determined not to let him see how Nick rattled her. "Be a good boy," she told Henry, "so you can get out of here." She squeezed his hand, then leaned down and kissed his cheek.

As she turned to leave, she ran smack into the speculation in Nick's eyes. Every thought of assertiveness, of self-confidence, flew right out of her head. Gracious, she'd forgotten how tall he was. At five-ten in heels, Sammi rarely had to look up to meet a man's gaze, even had to look down at a few. But her eyes barely reached this man's chin. She gave a mumbled, "Excuse me," brushed past Nick Elliott, and made what felt suspiciously like a harrowing escape.

Nick watched the door swing shut on silent hinges, then turned to Henry. "A playmate of yours?"

"That's not even remotely funny."

No, Nick thought. Nothing was ever funny around Henry.

"You remember her, don't you?"

Nick remembered Samantha Carmichael. How could he have forgotten a gorgeous Amazon like her? But he didn't remember this hot, hard, instant attraction he now felt. Didn't remember it, didn't want it. Resented the hell out of it.

In addition to that day in Henry's office, Nick had seen Samantha Carmichael a few times on his rare trips through the plant during the past couple of years. But he recalled a girl in jeans and sneakers hovering nervously by the coffee machine. Even pictured her in a welder's mask with a torch in her hand down in fabrication, welding an inlet duct for a Commander, fierce concentration etched on her face.

A knockout face, he thought now. But the girl had turned into a woman since he'd last seen her, a cool, haughty woman. She'd tamed that wild head of vibrant auburn hair into a sleek little knot at her nape. The denims had given way to the female version of a three-piece suit. A rather unflattering, ill-fitting suit.

Thinking about the sneakers she used to wear, he frowned. He wished she'd kept them. He didn't like the things he felt when he noticed what high heels did for her legs. Not to mention what they did for her height. He liked being able to look directly into her eyes when they spoke rather than having nothing to see but the top of her head.

Damned if he hadn't suddenly developed a weakness for tall women.

And how the hell could he have possibly forgotten that tiny mole at the corner of her mouth?

Did he remember Samantha Carmichael? If she hadn't crossed his mind much in the past couple of years, he knew without a doubt she was now permanently etched there, whether he wanted her there or not.

Henry was giving him an odd look. How long had he stood there thinking about Samantha Carmichael? "I remember her," Nick said.

Henry nodded slowly. "Good."

"So tell me, *Dad*. Just what does the Director of Advanced Technology do?"

Henry smiled. Nick couldn't remember the last time he'd seen Henry smile. The man settled against the pillows and cupped his hands behind his head. "She investigates the latest technology. New machines, methods, robotics, that sort of thing. She makes sure we're as efficient a factory as we can be."

Nick rolled his eyes. "And you felt the need to create a new position for her?"

Henry chuckled. "Special lady, special job."

"Why couldn't Manufacturing Engineering handle the job? Sounds like J. W.'s territory, to me."

"Humph. Truth is, J. W.'s too set in his ways. Why should I wait around for him to find the initiative Sammi's shown?"

"If he's lost his edge, maybe it's time to replace him."

19

"Now don't go jumping to conclusions," Henry warned. "J. W.'s too good at what he does to think about losing him. You just take your time. Don't make any snap decisions — about J. W. or Sammi."

Nick shrugged. "I assume the nester program was a good idea. What else has this 'special lady' done to earn this 'special job?'"

"Just read her file. I think you'll be impressed."

"We'll see."

"You're not going to give her a hard time, are you?"

Nick shrugged again. "Why would I do that?"

"If I knew why you do some of the things you do . . . Let's just say nothing you do surprises me."

"If she asks for a hard time, I'll give it to her. If she doesn't, I won't."

Henry eyed him a long moment, then nodded. "All right. Just be fair with her. She's only had the job two weeks."

Nick clenched his jaw to keep from saying what was on his mind. He had a company to run. Elliott manufactured aircraft parts and subassemblies for some of the giants in the aerospace industry. Giants like McDonnell Douglas, Boeing, Lockheed. Nick didn't have time for hand-holding.

He was due to take over Elliott Air tomorrow morning. And instead of being able to get down to business, it looked like the first thing he would have to deal with was a brand new director who probably didn't know what she was doing. If that wasn't bad enough, Nick knew without a doubt that he'd never been more intrigued in his life than he was by the shadows that seemed to lurk behind her cool facade.

That she was an employee and therefore, by his own rules, off-limits, scarcely fazed the mystery, the challenge she represented.

And if *that* wasn't bad enough, Samantha Carmichael gave every appearance of being Henry Elliott's mistress.

Two

The next morning the left turn light at Northwest Fiftieth and MacArthur turned red . . . as usual. Just in time to keep Sammi from making it through the intersection. While waiting for the green arrow, she ran her hand over the smooth burgundy leather of her new briefcase. Henry had given it to her a little over two weeks ago in honor of her new job.

It was so like Henry to give her a gift in honor of another of his gifts. That's how she thought of her new job—as a gift. From Henry, from heaven. She was almost as excited over the promotion as she was the huge salary increase. The bills that money would pay!

But what was she going to do without Henry? He had such faith in her, had encouraged her so much. She wondered if she had what it would take to do the work, and do it right, without Henry's reassuring presence. It was more than obvious she wasn't going to get much support from Nick Elliott.

The arrow turned green, and Sammi pressed the gas pedal. For a moment, nothing happened. *Not now, not now.* Behind her, a horn honked. She pressed the accelerator harder. After another lull, the old car finally jerked and wheezed its way through the intersection.

She couldn't help but remember the hard, speculative look in Nick Elliott's eyes yesterday. Such a cold blue. Like ice chips. So different from Henry's laughing gray eyes.

No, she'd get no support, probably not even much in the way of cooperation, from Nick. Not when he so obviously thought she and Henry had something going, which Henry had deliberately led him to believe. Sammi had tossed and turned half the night trying to figure out why Henry would do such a thing. She hadn't come up with a single logical reason, except that Henry and Nick were much better described as adversaries than father and son. Henry may have led Nick to think what he did just to aggravate him.

No matter what the reason, Sammi intended to put a stop to it. She didn't know the cause of their long-standing problems, but she was not about to be caught in the middle. She would go to Nick and tell him . . . Tell him what? That she was not involved with his father? Even to her mind, that sounded defensive. She could be wrong about what Nick was thinking. But she didn't believe she was. If she were, and she went to him denying something he wasn't even thinking, she'd look like an idiot. Or worse—she'd look guilty of the very thing she was denying.

She drove by Gulfstream, Elliott's next-door competitor, not that Elliott Air was big enough to cause one of the aerospace giants any sleepless nights. Then she passed the Elliott Air security gate. She didn't have to park in the back by the hangars anymore. Instead, she pulled into her reserved spot in front of Elliott's red brick office building.

No, she couldn't rush in denying something she wasn't sure she was even accused of. She would wait to see what happened. Who knew? Maybe Henry had straightened out the misconception after she left the hospital yesterday.

And maybe the world was flat. Henry had misled Nick on purpose. That much she knew. What she didn't know, couldn't even guess, was why.

She locked her car and headed for the building, eager to leave the ninety-plus August morning heat for the air-conditioned comfort indoors. A disadvantage of her new job was that business suits and pantyhose were a heck of a lot hotter and less comfortable than the jeans and T-shirts she'd worn in the shop.

But the work itself represented a challenge and was worth everything to her. It meant independence, security, a chance to prove herself. The salary meant a chance to pay off Jim's bills.

And if her office still resembled the former broom closet it once was, Sammi didn't care. She stared at the shiny brass nameplate on the door and smiled. Who would have thought the name Samantha Carmichael would ever grace an office door? Certainly not her.

See, Jim? I am a real person.

She opened the door and flipped on the light. Without it, the room was pitch-black. Former broom closets didn't come with windows. But that was all right with Sammi. Except sometimes, she could almost swear she heard Jim laughing.

Some big executive, eh, Sammi? You don't even rate a real office. You can still smell the floor cleaner they used to keep in here.

Sammi set her briefcase on the army-green file cabinet beside her gray steel desk. "Shut up, Jim. At least I'm alive, which is more than I can say for you." With a grimace, she glanced over her shoulder to make sure no one was in the hall to overhear her talking to herself.

She had to stop doing that, she reminded herself. Had to stop hearing Jim's voice, had to stop answering him. Jim had been dead for three years. He no longer had any power over her, as he'd had when they were married.

Somewhere deep down she understood that the only power Jim had ever had over her was the control she had unwittingly given him. But those days were over. She never intended to give anyone so much as one little ounce of power over her again. She supported herself, took care of herself, made her own decisions. She was her own person.

For the past three years since Jim's death, she had proved as much to herself daily.

Henry was the only person who had taken the time and trouble to look beneath her tough, cool act. He'd seen the vulnerable, insecure woman she'd been. But she had conquered her self-doubts long ago. Most of them, anyway. Now wasn't the time to remember the past. Nick would take control of Elliott Air today. *That* was something worth worrying about.

Sammi took a deep breath and sat down at her desk, then finally noticed the memo lying there. As new company president, Nick Elliott was calling a staff meeting for 8:30. Oh, boy. Her first staff meeting, and Henry wouldn't be present.

But that was all right. She didn't need Henry's support. It was just a meeting. She could handle it.

At 8:29 she stood outside the door to the conference room and let four people enter before her, then took a seat at the middle of the huge mahogany table. She was more nervous than she cared to admit.

The last person in was Nick Elliott. He and the other staff members greeted one another like long-lost buddies. Rounds of backslapping and handshaking and "Welcome home, Nick." The other executive staff members — Manufacturing, Manufacturing Engineering, Quality Control, Production, Marketing, Administration/Accounting, Service — had held their positions for several years. Sammi was the sole newcomer, as well as the only woman. The men gave her cautious nods and halfhearted smiles, but other than that, ignored her.

Nick finally took his seat and got down to business. "Thank you for dropping everything and coming on such short notice. I promise this won't take long. You all know why I'm here, that I'm taking over from Henry. He's doing fine, by the way. He'll be leaving the hospital today and going home."

"How permanent do you think his retirement is?" Vic Corely from Production asked.

Sammi frowned. As far as she knew, Henry's retirement was for real. Vic had a point, though. Henry could always change his mind. But looking at Nick, knowing the adversarial relationship he and Henry had, Sammi didn't think changing his mind about retiring would do Henry any good. Those steely blue eyes of Nick's said that once he got his hands on something he wanted, Nick Elliott would never let go.

The thing Sammi didn't know was how badly Nick wanted Elliott Air. He'd certainly not shown any interest in the home office while Henry had been in charge.

"Henry won't be coming back," Nick said. "The paperwork is underway now naming me president."

So, he wanted the company. The idea of facing this man every work day unsettled her.

27

"I just thought all of you should know that while I don't anticipate making any drastic changes immediately, keep in mind I'm not Henry. There probably will be changes down the road, some you might like, some you might not."

Why did those blue eyes zero in on her with that last comment? Sammi's heart pounded. What did he have in store for her?

"That's really all I have to say for now. I'd like to talk with each of you individually sometime today. Let Marie know when you can spare me about a half hour."

The meeting broke up at once. As the "good-ol'-boy" network fired up again with talk of ball games and fishing and "Hey, remember the time . . . ," Sammi left the conference room and went back to her office. She had worried for nothing. The meeting had been simple, quick, and to the point. The only thing that bothered her was why Nick had chosen that precise moment, when he'd hinted at unpleasant changes, to look at her. She sure could have done without that.

She could also do without a private session with her new boss, but she knew she couldn't avoid it. Maybe during their meeting she'd be able to learn what interpretation he had put on Henry's game yesterday in the hospital.

Sometime today she needed to check the latest figures from Production. Last week's numbers indicated the new Computerized Numerically

28

Controlled Router was doing as she predicted — increasing production.

But first she would schedule her meeting with Nick. She squared her shoulders and took the hall to the opposite end of the building. Henry's end.

No. Nick's end.

She stopped at his secretary's desk. "Hi, Marie. I need to schedule an appointment with Nick."

Marie smiled and waved a hand. "He's free now. Go right on in."

"Now?"

Marie winked. "You can be first."

First. Great. Sammi swallowed a protest. "Fine."

She turned toward his office and fought the urge to wipe her palms on her skirt. The gesture would be entirely too telling. That her hands were sweating at all made her angry. She hadn't felt this unsure of herself since her first meeting with Henry. Her heels striking the floor sounded like gunshots. She paused at the open door and looked in. Nick sat in the tall-backed leather chair behind his big mahogany desk, the phone pressed to his ear. He saw her and waved her in.

While he finished his conversation, Sammi took a seat in one of the two chairs facing the desk and lectured herself. This unsettled feeling she had around Nick Elliott was completely without cause. He was her boss, not her executioner. She was an asset to Elliott Air. A loyal, hardworking employee. She lived and breathed Elliott Air.

Stop that. She had no need to reassure herself. Nick probably just wanted to know what projects she was working on, how her job was going, the usual stuff. There was no earthly reason for her to be nervous. Nick Elliott was not a monster. He was merely the new president of the company.

So why were her fingers entwined more intricately than a French braid?

She tried not to stare as he talked on the phone and quoted figures from a report on his desk, but her gaze kept straying to his mouth. He had a very expressive mouth. Firm and grim one minute, relaxed and smiling the next. And when he pursed his lips in thought, his eyes narrowed.

Then he swiped at those lips with his tongue. That's when Sammi became aware that her pounding heart had nothing to do with Nick the boss and everything to do with Nick the man. With a quick intake of breath, she imagined what those lips would feel like on hers.

Then she called herself six kinds of a fool. If she ever again decided to let any man get close enough to kiss her, it sure wouldn't be this man. No more domineering, browbeating types for her. And if ever such an individual walked the earth, his name was surely Nick Elliott.

He finished his call and hung up the phone. Sammi schooled her thoughts and her expression.

Nick leaned back in his chair and looked at her through narrowed eyes. "Funny," he said softly, "I wouldn't have thought you'd be first."

While wondering what in the world he meant by that, Sammi managed at tight smile. "Just lucky, I guess."

He studied her a moment longer—long enough to make her want to fidget—then he appeared to relax. "Henry seems . . . to have a lot of faith in you."

Embarrassed, and not sure why, Sammi glanced away. "I guess he does."

"I hope it's not misplaced."

Suddenly feeling like a cornered rabbit and not liking the feeling one bit, she raised her head as high as it would go. "I don't believe it is."

"I have to be honest with you, Sammi. It is all right that I call you Sammi, isn't it?"

She nodded.

"I'm not questioning your ability to do your job."

She stared at him. "You're not?"

Nick shrugged. "Not exactly."

Alarm bells went off in her head. "Then what are you questioning? Exactly."

"I'm questioning the need for the job at all."

Sammi felt her mouth go dry. The oatmeal she'd had for breakfast churned. "Are you firing me?"

"No," Nick said slowly. "But I am adhering to current company policy and putting you on ninety-day probation."

"Probation? But I've worked here three years."

"Not in this job, you haven't."

Sammi swallowed the bile that threatened to choke her and concentrated on controlling her shaking hands. "What . . ." She swallowed again. "What is it you expect of me during the next three months?"

"Performance. Results. Proof that your job is vital and that you're the right person to do it."

Anger burned her cheeks. "You think I don't earn my pay?"

Nick shrugged. "Prove me wrong."

"And if I don't, I'm fired. Right?"

"Your record in production is impressive. If this job doesn't work out, I'd rather see you go back to the shop than leave the company."

Go back to the shop. And let everyone know she'd failed.

"Understand, Sammi, I'm not judging you."

She bit back a harsh laugh. "Aren't you?"

"No. What I'm really doing is questioning Henry's decision to create this job in the first place."

She took a slow deep breath to ease her trembling. That's all she needed—to become the latest bone of contention between Henry and his son. And as the president of Elliott Air, in charge of every aspect of running the operation, Nick would win this round. "Is there anything else?"

"No, that pretty much covers things."

No kidding. She gave him a sharp nod. "Then I guess I'd better get to work." She rose without waiting for an answer and headed for the door.

"I hope this doesn't put too much pressure on you."

Sammi paused in the doorway and gave him a look over her shoulder. "Pressure? You've just told me I have ninety days to prove I'm effective in a job you think is unnecessary. Why on earth would you think I'd feel any pressure?"

Nick stared at the open doorway Sammi had just vacated. At least now he wouldn't have to worry about how to deal with his attraction to her. That iceberg look of hers would give him frostbite if he got too close. She hadn't even flinched when he'd put her on probation.

What was it about this particular woman that intrigued him? He liked his women petite, he thought with a grin. Docile. Loving. Warm. He'd never been attracted to the cool, aloof type before. Neither had Henry, for that matter. Yet when Sammi Carmichael had looked at Henry yesterday in the hospital, she'd been anything but cool. She'd been open and warm and smiling.

Would she ever look at Nick that way?

Hell, no. And he didn't want her to. He straightened in his chair. He had a company to run, and he wasn't about to compete with Henry for a woman, especially one who worked for him.

Maybe if she didn't have that sexy little mole at the corner of her mouth . . . if he hadn't seen her tongue come out and touch it while he was on the

33

phone, hadn't imagined touching it himself, tasting it . . .

Hellfire. He didn't have room in his life for unreasonable fantasies, and that's just what Sammi Carmichael was. That, plus his employee—which put her off-limits—plus whatever she was to Henry. Nick didn't want to be attracted to her. He wouldn't be. She wasn't his type at all. Besides, he'd just threatened her job. She wouldn't want anything to do with him.

Which was just how things should be. To hell with the way his blood rushed whenever he thought of her.

The company came first, and Nick still saw no valid reason for Sammi's position to exist. Henry had told him to look in her file, and Nick had done so first thing that morning. All it contained were employment statistics and a few compliments from her supervisor on the floor. Did Henry think that would impress him?

Her file said she was from Stillwater. With Oklahoma State University right there in her hometown, why didn't she have a college degree? Nick would be damned if he would fork out a top salary just because Henry liked her.

Thinking of Henry, Nick pushed his chair back and got up. It was time to do his "familial" duty and go bail the old buzzard out of the hospital.

Ninety days. He'd said she had ninety days. But

Sammi knew Nick Elliott had already made up his mind about her. As far as he was concerned, she and her job were superfluous. How was she supposed to function with his threat hanging over her head?

"I hope this doesn't put too much pressure on you," she mimicked.

Ha. He didn't care what kind pressure he put on her, he just wanted to get rid of her. And he would get his wish, too. But she wasn't about to give him the satisfaction of yanking her job out from under her. The next move would be hers. And move, she would.

She had three months to find a new job.

Yeah, some big executive, eh, Sammi? How long did the job last—two weeks?

That voice! Jim's voice. Why wouldn't he go away and leave her alone? She had enough problems without his constant taunting, his ever present reminders of the person she used to be. She wasn't that person any longer. She was strong and independent. At least, more so than she had been with Jim.

She certainly had enough mettle to survive hunting for a new job.

For the time being, she would carry on as though nothing was wrong. She went downstairs to Production and delved through their records, talked to employees, then spent a great part of her time collating the data and typing the report she would present to Nick on the new CNC Router.

Late in the afternoon Henry called.

"So how was your first day with a new boss?"

"It was okay." She wasn't about to tell Henry the truth. If he learned about her probation, it wouldn't be from her. She would not lean on him. It was her problem; she would handle it herself. "How is your first day home from the hospital?"

"Heaven," he claimed. "It's good to be out of that place. It felt like I'd been there a year."

Sammi responded to the smile in his voice with a smile of her own. "I know you're going to get sick of this question real fast, but, are you taking it easy?"

"Honey, if I moved any slower, you'd think I was in a coma."

"How did you get home?"

There was a slight pause before he said, "Nick brought me." He sounded . . . surprised.

Sammi wasn't going to touch that. "Is Mrs. Simms looking after you?"

"That woman," he said with a growl. "For a housekeeper, she's getting way out of hand."

Sammi laughed. "She's a very nice lady and you know it."

"She's a witch. She's treating me like a helpless invalid. One short afternoon, and she's already driving me crazy. I need rescuing, Sammi. How about coming over Saturday? I can't swim, but you could. Then we could have a nice long visit over lunch."

Henry was lonely. She heard it in his voice. She,

36

too, was lonely, she admitted to herself. Besides, she'd like to talk to him about the way he had acted at the hospital when Nick had arrived, why he had deliberately led Nick to think things that weren't true. Saturday would be the perfect time. "That sounds good. About ten?"

"Fine. See you then. And I expect you to tell me everything that's been happening at the plant."

"Now, Henry—"

"Don't you 'now Henry' me. I'm not in danger of keeling over dead at your feet if you talk about work. You and Nick are both being ridiculous."

So, Nick wasn't discussing the company. Then surely he hadn't told Henry about putting her on probation. She felt some of the tension in her shoulders ease. "Henry, Henry," she teased. "What are we going to do with you?"

"You're going to come over here Saturday in a skimpy bikini and let me ogle your limbs."

"Ogle my what?" Sammi laughed and turned to pick up her coffee cup. "Henry, you know I don't own a bikini." Her hand froze halfway to her cup. Leaning against her doorjamb was Nick Elliott. The knowing smirk on his face told her he'd heard what she had just said.

Oblivious to Sammi's predicament, Henry said, "Limbs. You know, legs, arms? And you should own a bikini. Sammi? You still there?"

"Uh . . . yes." She looked away from Nick. "I'm here."

"You sound funny. Is something wrong?"

Wrong? What could possibly be wrong? "No, nothing."

"You'll be here Saturday then, at ten?"

"Yes."

She was reluctant to end the conversation and face Nick, but Henry said goodbye and hung up. The need to explain, to defend herself was strong, but before she could even think what to say, Nick spoke.

"After yesterday, I suspected, but now I know for certain how you got this job."

She turned to face him, her stomach clenched in a painful knot. "No," she said, "you don't know."

One eyebrow arched. "Don't I?" he asked.

Assertive. She had to be assertive. She set her jaw. "I'm a plain-speaking person, Mr. Elliott. If you've got something to say, or something you'd like to ask, why don't you just come out with it?"

Nick pulled away from the door and stuffed his hands into his pockets. "Don't try to kid me, *Ms* Carmichael. You know exactly what I'm thinking."

"Why don't you tell me?"

He shook his head slowly. "No, I don't think so. If you're going to work here, what I'm thinking is better left unsaid."

He looked around the room, his expression turning into a frown of irritation as he scanned her cubbyhole. "I just came from Production. I understand you're the one responsible for that new computerized router."

The abrupt change of topic left Sammi reeling. One minute he threatened her job, then he as much as accused her of having an affair with his father. Now he was down to business. She took a deep breath to keep from screaming. "I suggested the CNC Router, yes."

"How much did it set us back?"

"The total price was right at a million dollars."

Nick pursed his lips. "Do you understand the term 'return on investment'?"

It was all Sammi could do to keep from rolling her eyes. Did he think she was a complete imbecile? How the devil did he think she'd gotten this far without understanding a term like that?

But then, Nick had his own ideas as to how she got her job. She couldn't add fuel to the fire by screaming at him, so she kept her voice as even as possible. "The ROI in my proposal was three years."

"And will we make it?"

"Yes."

"You seem pretty sure of yourself."

"I'm sure of that machine." She picked up the report she'd just finished and handed it to him. "When you read this, you'll realize that if the production figures maintain their current level, the ROI will come in as much as six months early."

"Why did we need a second router?"

"To increase production."

That finally shut him up, but only for a minute. "And you keep track of the figures?"

"That's my job."

Nick nodded. "Fine. See that you do it."

Oooo! If she had the nerve, she'd throw her coffee cup at his head! But he didn't wait around to give her the chance. Simply walked out and left her sitting there so mad she wanted to spit. See that you do it, indeed. "I'll do my job, *Mr.* Elliott. At least until I find another one."

See that you do it. Ha. She had a good mind to forget about finding a different job. She ought to stick around Elliott Air, if for no other reason than to give the president a permanent case of heartburn.

Three

At ten o'clock Saturday morning, Sammi pulled into the front circle drive of Henry's massive, gray brick house. The sweet scent of fresh-cut Bermuda grass floated through the exclusive Quail Creek neighborhood on the hot southern breeze. Sammi inhaled and savored the smell. Childhood summer vacations. The coughing drone of her father's old lawn mower. Green-stained feet.

Funny how none of the memories evoked by the scent of cut grass were recent. Surely she had noticed the fragrance when Jim had mowed. Or rather, when Jim had hired someone else to trim the lawn. But there in Henry's driveway, she couldn't recall a single instance in her ten-year marriage when she had stopped to enjoy the sweet aroma.

"Enough of this."

She grabbed her straw bag and got out of the car. Before she reached the porch, Henry opened the front door and grinned a welcome. He looked good, she thought. Better than she had expected, considering his recent heart attack.

He gave her a dramatic sigh. "No bikini, huh?"

Sammi glanced down at her T-shirt and jeans, then grinned. "Sorry."

Henry snapped his fingers. "I've got it—you're swimming nude." He wiggled his eyebrows.

"Your pool would dry up in protest."

"Sammi, Sammi, we have to do something about this negative self-image of yours. We licked it at work, but the personal side of the issue still needs attention."

"What we have to do," Sammi said brushing past him into the cool dimness of the entry hall, "is change the subject. How are you feeling?"

"I'm feeling great. How are things at the plant?"

"They're fine."

"You and Nick getting along okay?"

It took considerable effort to keep from grinding her teeth at the mention of Nick's name. "We're getting along fine."

"How's he treating you?"

"Fine."

"Fine. Fine. Everything's fine. You're not going to tell me a thing, are you?"

"There's nothing to tell. I've been working—"

"Did you get the latest figures on the new router?"

Sammi rolled her eyes. "Yes, Henry."

"Are they as good as the last set?"

"Yes, Henry."

"I'm being a pest, aren't I?"

Sammi smiled. "Yes, Henry."

He shook his head. "All right, I give up. I'll tell Mrs. Simms you're here. She'll fix lunch while you swim."

Sammi kissed him on the cheek. "You're a pal. I'll go change."

"You know your way to the guest room."

Henry headed for the kitchen, Sammi to the spare room. She changed into her plain, black maillot, dismayed at the low neck and high, French-cut thighs. It hadn't seemed so revealing when she'd bought it on sale last month.

She slipped on sandals and a terry cloth cover-up and headed back down the hall, through the den, and out the sliding patio doors. A few minutes after ten in the morning, and according to the thermometer on the wall beside the door, the temperature was already ninety-two. Just the thought of how hot it would be by midafternoon made the smooth blue water of the pool look more inviting than ever.

Henry's entire backyard had always been a favorite spot of Sammi's. The eight-foot-high redwood fence, with its partial cover of English ivy and climbing roses, enclosed the yard and pool in an air of seclusion. The emerald-green grass was always just the right height, not too tall, but not cropped to the ground. And never, in all the times Sammi had been there, had she seen a weed.

Whiskey barrels and all shapes of terra-cotta and glazed pots sat in various-sized groupings along the outer edge of the concrete apron around the pool. From each petunias, periwinkles, pansies, and marigolds spilled forth in a riot of blues and pinks and whites and golds.

At the far corner of the garden stood a magnificent silver maple, its dark green leaves rustling in the stiff hot wind.

The patio was the more formal end of the yard, with its glass-topped table and thickly cushioned chairs surrounded by redwood planters filled with perfectly trimmed boxwood topiaries. And here, too, was an abundance of flowers.

Sammi took it all in at a glance, then focused on her favorite spot—the pool.

Quickly she stepped out of her sandals and cover-up. Hot concrete burned her feet. She dove into the clear blue water. It shocked her with its coldness, but only for an instant. Before she took a full stroke toward the surface, the numbness was gone and she reveled in the cool, silky freedom. Just her and the water. As she broke the surface, a bubble of pleasure rose inside her.

Swimming was the one thing in life at which she had always excelled. In the water she had always felt an independence, a self-confidence she had lacked in most other areas of her life until going to work at Elliott Air. The water was her friend.

"How is it?" Henry called from the patio.

The water, her job, and Henry. Her three best friends.

She treaded water and turned toward the house, ignoring the sting of chlorine in her eyes. "It's terrific! I'm going to do a few laps."

"Only a few?"

She laughed with Henry. He knew her well. Last summer she had practically lived in his pool every chance she got, and most of that time was spent doing laps. She liked to drive herself to her physical limits and beyond by pushing harder and harder each time she swam.

With another laugh of sheer exhilaration, she took a stroke, eager for the burning muscles and gasping breath that told her she was alive.

Nick pulled into Henry's driveway dreading the confrontation sure to come. No matter how innocuous their conversations began, he and Henry invariably ended up arguing about something. Or nothing. This time there would be a serious issue. Nick felt obligated, although he had no idea why, to tell Henry about putting Samantha Carmichael on ninety-day probation.

Of course, all Nick's dread about telling Henry was probably for nothing. It was likely he already knew. Unless Nick missed his guess, the

45

woman in question had surely already gone running to Henry.

He could hear her now. "Big bad Nicky told me I have to *work,* Henry-poo. You'll just have to straighten him out."

To be fair, Ms Carmichael didn't seem as bad as all that, but she and Henry were obviously involved. Surely she had told the old man what Nick had done. He had been expecting an irate phone call for the past two days.

That was primarily why he had driven over to the house. He was tired of waiting for the explosion. Better to get it over with now, in private, and be done with this particular argument.

He stepped out of the car into the humid heat, wondering who could have parked the twenty-year-old, peeling green Ford in Henry's driveway. So much for the privacy Nick had hoped for. The rusted clunker certainly wasn't up to Mrs. Simms' standards, nor did it look like the type of car driven by any of Henry's friends. The thing looked like one good kick would tumble it into pieces. Maybe Henry had hired a yardman.

Nick stepped onto the porch and rang the bell. A moment later Mrs. Simms opened the door. She gave him a brief smile. "Mr. Elliott is out on the patio." She stepped back and gestured him inside. "Will you be staying for lunch?"

Knowing what eating with Henry did to his digestion, Nick shook his head. "No, thanks."

"He's got a pitcher of tea with him. I'll bring you a glass."

"Thanks." Nick went through to the den and slid open the patio door. For a man who hadn't been out of the hospital a week yet, Henry looked good.

It wasn't until Nick stepped onto the covered patio and closed the glass door behind him that he noticed the long, slim figure smoothly skimming the length of the pool. He watched for a full minute as the woman's strong strokes took her from one end to the other, and back again. He might have watched forever, fascinated by the supple movement of feminine muscles, the exacting precision of each graceful stroke . . .

Might have, but Henry interrupted with a brusque, "Good morning. What are you doing here?"

"Good morning to you, too." Nick slowly looked away from the mermaid in black and turned toward Henry. As he did so, the identity of the woman struck him. If that wasn't Samantha Carmichael—every startlingly glorious inch of her—in that pool, his name wasn't Nick Elliott.

Henry sat at the glass-topped table sipping iced tea and eyeing Nick curiously. Nick took the cushioned chair across from him, wondering where Henry's usual look of hostility was. For one startling instant, Nick wondered—*What if it*

*had never been there? What if, in my own pain,
I only imagined it? What if he really . . .*

Nick shifted in his chair. He'd never imagined
a damned thing, and he knew it. If Henry suddenly chose to appear pleasant after twenty years
of animosity, there was surely a calculated reason. Maybe the heart attack had mellowed him
out, but Nick doubted it. The image of a mellow
Henry did not fit with the man Nick had known
all his life.

"Just slumming?" Henry asked. "Or are you
here for a reason?"

Mrs. Simms came out and poured Nick a glass
of tea. Ice cubes clinked and cracked, an odd ac-
companiment to the rhythmic splashes from the
pool and the sounds of children playing coming
from somewhere down the street.

"I came for a reason, but it looks like she beat
me to it."

Henry raised a brow. "She?"

"Your . . . friend in the pool."

"Sammi? You came to see me about Sammi?"

Nick took a sip of tea, savoring the coolness
on his tongue. "I figured she would have already
told you. I put her on probation."

"You *what?*"

The rhythmic splashing in the pool faltered,
then resumed.

"She didn't tell you? Standard ninety-day probation due any employee in a new job."

Henry stared at him a moment, the curiosity

in his eyes replaced by the more familiar hostility. "So she has to prove herself to you in three months or you'll throw her out, is that it?"

"That's company policy." Nick took another sip of tea.

Henry slammed his glass down. "Hell, Sammi doesn't need to prove herself, damn it. I ought to put you on ninety-day probation."

"You can't. I'm the president."

Henry leaned forward. "But I own the company."

Sammi heard voices. Had Henry turned on the radio? The angry shout told her no. She lost her concentration for a moment. Someone other than Henry was on the patio. She should stop and get out of the pool.

In this suit? No way. She'd stay in the water and keep swimming until whoever it was went away. She kicked out and found her rhythm again. She had long ago lost count of her laps. She wasn't swimming for numbers, but for the sheer exhilaration of discovering how far she could push herself. Nowhere else did she feel confident enough to test her limits but in the water.

She swam toward what runners called "the wall"—that point of physical exhaustion when each step came harder and slower, until the runner knew the next stride would be impossible.

She didn't know what swimmers called it, but she supposed "wall" was as appropriate a term as any.

With each stroke her muscles screamed louder, burned hotter. She felt restrained, as though someone had grabbed her legs and was holding her back. Her arms weighed at least a ton. Each kick grew slower, each breath more gasping, the end of the pool farther away.

She forgot about Henry's unknown visitor, about her troubles at work, the debts Jim had left. She forgot her curious attraction for and teeth-gnashing frustration with Nick Elliott. She forgot everything as she concentrated totally on completing one more stroke. Then another.

Then she hit it. The imaginary wall. She could not force her arm over her head one more time, not for all she was worth. But she did. Once, twice, three times. And then, like a caged bird set free, she burst through the heaviness and exhaustion and shot down the length of the pool.

She'd done it! She didn't care how many laps she made, so long as she crossed the barrier. Next time she would test herself further by pushing until every last ounce of her strength left her. Today she would merely enjoy a few more laps.

Several more lengths of the pool were executed at a leisurely, Sunday-driver kind of pace. As she made the final approach of the deep end, she reached for the side and used the momentum of one last kick to propel her up and out of the water. Her quivering arms collapsed, and she fell back, laughing.

When she surfaced, Henry was laughing from the other end of the pool. "Want me to call in a crane to hoist you out of there?"

"Not —" She gasped. "— yet."

Twice more she tried to lift herself. Both times her arms gave out. Sammi laughed again. "God, I'm limp. Bring on the crane."

Henry chuckled. "Naw, I think I'll just leave you there. I kind of like you with that pruney look."

"Thanks." She turned and swam slowly toward the steps at the shallow end of the pool. "You're a real . . ." The sight of Nick sitting across the table from Henry made her forget for a moment what she'd been saying. What was he doing there?

"A real pal," she finally managed.

Steel-blue eyes watched her every movement, making her excruciatingly self-conscious. It was bad enough that she felt like a drowned rat, with her sopping hair coming out of its ponytail and streaming down her face and across her shoulders and back. But to be half-naked, too, was more than she cared to deal with in front of this man.

Would he leave soon? She wondered how long she could stay in the water without raising questions.

Not long, it seemed, for Henry rose and

walked to the intercom unit by the door. "Sammi's out now, Mrs. Simms. We'll take lunch in about fifteen minutes, after she catches her breath. Oh, and make it for three, please. Nick will be staying."

Nick will be staying. Great. There was no help for it. As Sammi walked up the shallow end of the pool, the water fell away from her, exposing her inch by inch to that hard-eyed stare. No matter what, she would not tug on her swimsuit.

She took the steps out of the pool, feeling as though she weighed a ton after the weightlessness of the water. Her knees quivered and threatened to buckle. Her breath came fast. The wind she knew was hot felt cold against her wet skin. Without bothering to dry off first, she reached for the terry cloth cover-up and whipped it on. Then, with her back to the men, she used the towel to squeeze as much water as possible from her tangled hair.

What was Nick doing here?

Slowly she turned and walked toward the table, carrying the towel before her like a shield. "Hello, Nick."

He nodded. As his gaze inched over her from head to toe, chasing her chill away, replacing it with a disconcerting heat, his lips twitched. "Sammi."

Her heartbeat should have slowed by now. What was it about this man that unnerved her so? Yes, he was ruggedly handsome, but she had always liked a more refined look. And since Jim's death, she preferred no look at all. She wasn't interested in any man.

So what if his dark hair seemed like a woman had just run her fingers through it? Why should she care if the blue cotton pullover exactly matched his eyes, or that his worn jeans, so different from the expensive business suits he normally wore, hugged his thighs like a second skin?

None of that should affect her. Neither should the shape of his lips, but she was honest enough with herself to admit it did. Now *there* was a problem. She liked her boss's mouth.

Don't be foolish, Sammi. He's not the least interested in you, no matter what you think you see in his eyes.

"Here." Henry held out a chair for her. "Sit down and rest."

"I, uh, I think I should go," she told him. "You two probably have a lot to talk about."

"Nonsense." Henry gave her a slight push toward the cushioned seat. "I invited you for lunch, you're staying for lunch. Nick, too."

Sammi forced a shrug and sat down.

Henry took his place again. "How many laps did you do?"

Appearing calm and sure of herself was difficult, to put it mildly, while Nick continued staring at her. She turned toward Henry. "I didn't count."

"Our Sammi, here, swims like a fish," Henry told Nick.

There he went again, with his "our Sammi" cracks. And she hadn't even had the chance to talk to him about what had gone on in front of Nick at the hospital the last time the three of them had been together.

"So I noticed," Nick said.

She could still feel his gaze on her. How was she supposed to catch her breath?

"Only I'd say she was more like a mermaid," Nick added.

Sammi refused to comment, or to look at him. She helped herself to some tea and gulped it down. Feeling awkward and gauche, she set the glass carefully on the table and folded her hands in her lap.

Nick watched her fidget with the tie of her cover-up. So the lady wasn't as cool and collected as she would have him think. The hot color in her cheeks added to his conviction.

And those legs. No woman with legs that long, with a body as lush as hers, had any business being an ice maiden. Surely Henry found some warmth beneath that surface. She certainly managed to generate some heat in Nick, heat he was doing his level best to ignore. Did Henry react the same way to her?

The thought of Henry and Sammi together left a sourness in his throat that tasted precariously like jealousy and made Nick furious. He'd be damned if he would be envious of his own — of Henry.

Look at the old goat, patting her hand and grinning at her like an idiot. And look at her smile back, as if Henry Elliott was the greatest thing that ever lived.

When was the last time a woman had gazed at Nick that way?

The question startled him. He didn't want a woman to look at him like that. It spoke of closeness, of shared thoughts and secrets. Nick didn't share those things with anyone. He liked his relationships, business and personal, to remain casual. His women should be petite and dainty and hanging on his every word. He had never been attracted to tall ice maidens, and he'd be damned if he'd start now.

He shoved his chair back and stood up. "I've got to go."

Henry gave him a thoughtful glance. This was where the old man usually came across with something scathing. "No comment?" Nick asked.

Henry merely shrugged. "Suit yourself. You always do."

"Right." Nick nodded to Henry, then Sammi, and left by the side gate. In the driveway he stopped beside the run-down Ford. Sammi's car, he assumed. Hell, with her salary she could certainly afford something that gave at least the appearance of reliability, not to mention paint.

As he started past the green bomb, something caught his eye. He leaned down and peered through the open passenger window. On the front seat lay the classifieds. He reached in and picked the pages up. Today's issue, and three "help wanted" ads bore red circles.

Apparently she wasn't going to wait for her ninety-day evaluation. It surprised him somehow. He had thought of Samantha Carmichael as many things. Cool, self-assured, even grasping. But he'd never thought of her as a quitter.

For the rest of the weekend and into the next week Nick tried to ignore the thought that Sammi was looking for another job. It was no skin off his nose if she left.

Still, he couldn't put it out of his mind. What if he had misjudged her? What if she was leaving because of his attitude?

No, she was probably going because she knew her job was superfluous. Because she would never be able to wrap him around her little finger the way she had Henry.

So why did it bother him?

He thought about talking to her about it, but every time he got within shouting distance, she hustled off to some other part of the plant. Which was probably just as well, because aside from remembering those want ads on her car seat, he couldn't help remembering how she'd

56

looked rising slowly from the pool, water cascading off her golden skin, her lashes heavy with droplets, her chest heaving with effort, her lips wet and glistening.

Damn it, he had to quit thinking about her. She was Henry's, for crying out loud.

Thunder rumbled outside the building. Surprised, Nick looked up to see rain beating against his window. He hadn't noticed the weather until then. He also hadn't noticed it was seven-thirty, and the offices were long since deserted. He stared at the storm, thinking he should go home and get something to eat.

The glass panes magnified the raindrops that clung there, reminding him of the single drop of water that had clung to and magnified that tiny mole at the corner of Sammi's mouth three days ago at Henry's.

"Enough."

He would go eat dinner. Maybe a good soaking on the way to his car would clear his head.

He locked his office behind him. The hall was lit but deserted. His footsteps down the tiled floor gave off a lonely echo. He'd never thought of the deserted offices as lonely before. No, it was something else. Himself? Was he lonely?

Nonsense.

Even if it were true, he didn't have time to worry about something so ridiculous. He had a company to run.

Still, he wondered if Henry ever missed the

closeness the two of them had shared, back when they had called each other father and son?

Father and son. So long ago. Yet, that day in Henry's hospital room, Henry had introduced Nick to Sammi as his son. Why, when Henry hadn't used that word in more than twenty years? Maybe Henry was lonely after all.

With a woman like Sammi? Not likely. With her, a man would never be lonely.

"Enough of her, damn it."

Nick stepped out the front door of the reception area onto the sidewalk. Earlier in the day the temperature had been in the upper nineties, but the storm had changed that. If he had to guess, he would put money on it now not being a degree above seventy. But the torrent had slackened to a light drizzle. He wasn't going to get that soaking he had thought he needed, the one that would take his mind off Sammi Carmichael.

He was wondering what she might be doing on a rainy evening like this when he heard the unmistakable sound of a car trying—and failing—to start. The miserable cranking whine bounced from one surrounding building to the next, a peculiarly plaintive echo in the stormy gray light.

Then he spotted her. Sammi. Sitting alone in her beat-up old car, all the parking spaces around her long since deserted.

Crank, crank, crank.

She was going to run her battery down.

Crank, craaank, crannnk . . . click, click . . . click.

Correction. She *had* run her battery down.

Four

The battery gave a final click, then nothing. Sammi leaned her head against the steering wheel and swore she would not cry. It was only a dead battery. Not important enough to get worked up over. Just because she was alone in the parking lot in the rain, in semidarkness, eight miles from home, with a car that wouldn't start and not a soul she could call for help except a cab, which she couldn't afford . . . No, nothing to get worked up over.

Damn!

Taking care of yourself just fine, aren't you, Sammi?

"Shut up, Jim. I can handle this."

Of course she could. With any luck at all, her jumper cables were in the trunk, if her neighbor had returned them last winter, which Sammi couldn't remember him doing. As for a running engine, all she had to do was go to the shop. Someone on the late shift would give her a boost.

She hated to ask for help, though. It made

her feel incompetent, as though she couldn't manage her own life. But this time, she had no choice.

She pulled on the door handle and shoved, but the car door stuck. She shoved again. Nothing. "Third time's charmed." While pulling on the handle again, she hit the door hard with her left shoulder. The door flew open. The handle ripped out of her grasp and took the tips of two nails with it, clear down to the quick, if the pain in her fingertips was any indication. Momentum sent her tilting sideways, directly toward the pavement. Her forehead connected with the arm rest, then slipped past it as her head rushed toward the ground. She barely caught herself in time, and even then, only by bracing her hand in a puddle of muddy water and bruising her palm on a pebble.

Thoroughly disgusted, cursing under her breath, Sammi straightened and yanked her keys from the ignition.

Way to go, Sam.

"Go to hell, Jim," she muttered. Then she winced. Knowing Jim better since his death than she ever had when he was alive, she feared hell was exactly where he had ended up.

Muttering a quick prayer for forgiveness, for herself and him, she got out of the car, careful to avoid the puddle, and walked around to the trunk. The wind made her shiver. Her head ached. With wet muddy fingers, she massaged the future bruise just above her left eye.

When she opened the trunk lid, the light was out of course. By the dim glow of the parking lot lights, she leaned in and searched for her jumper cables.

"Damn. Not here."

"If you're looking for the engine, you might try the other end."

The deep voice from out of the gray drizzle startled her. She jerked up and whacked the back of her head on the trunk lid. "Ow!"

"Sorry," Nick said. "I thought for sure you heard me coming."

Sammi backed carefully away from the car before straightening. With one hand rubbing fiercely at the pain on her skull that would likely turn into a giant lump any minute, she glared at Nick.

Sammi didn't get angry often. Probably because she normally didn't have the nerve. Plus, losing her temper usually left her feeling foolish. Why she should care about that at the moment was beyond her. She couldn't possibly look more ridiculous than she already did. Her clothes were damp and mussed, the rain had frizzed her hair, she'd nearly landed on her head beside her car — which Nick had obviously seen — and now she was jumping like a goose at the sound of his voice. Why should she worry about looking more foolish?

Nick struck a casual stance with feet spread

and his suit jacket bunched over where his hands disappeared into his pants pockets. That he ignored the rain, further loosened Sammi's tenuous hold on civility. All week she'd been dodging him, unwilling for him to mention her swimming at Henry's last Saturday. Now here he stood, relaxed, head cocked curiously to one side as though he'd never seen her before. And he was gorgeous. Drop-dead, rugged, masculine gorgeous, which she had no business noticing. And at which her heart had no business speeding up.

With clenched jaw, she asked, "What are you doing here?"

"I heard your battery give up the ghost and thought you might need some help."

"Oh." It was hard to be peevish to a man offering assistance. "Thanks."

Nick grinned. "I'll get my car."

Just then headlights cut across the parking lot. They caught on Sammi and Nick and held there, while the rumble of what had to be Gus Womak's pickup drew closer.

"Gus is coming," Sammi said. "He'll know what to do. But thanks anyway."

Gus pulled his black-and-chrome Ranger nose to nose with Sammi's car and climbed out. "Heard you out here grinding away," he hollered. "Thought you could use these." He waved a set of jumper cables over his head.

"Thanks, Gus," Sammi called. And she

meant it. As the shift foreman when she had worked on the line, Gus had always been good to her. He had taught her and encouraged her from the day she came to work. When she had new ideas she thought would benefit the company, he had insisted she take them straight to Henry.

Three weeks ago Gus had been so pleased with her promotion, he'd thrown an impromptu party in the parking lot at the end of their shift. Frankly, she had expected trouble rather than congratulations from him, for it wasn't often an employee was promoted over her supervisor.

And here he was again, riding through the rain to her rescue. *Yes,* she thought, *thanks, Gus.*

To Nick she said, "Thanks again. Good night."

She stepped around him and went to pop the hood of the Ford. Gus quickly raised it and his, then clamped on the jumper cables. He climbed back into his pickup and revved the engine. "Go ahead!" he hollered above the roar. "Crank her up!"

Sammi turned to get into her car and almost bumped into Nick. He put his hands on her arms to catch her. Tingling heat radiated from his touch. She jerked away. "Excuse me."

"My fault." Nick stepped back and opened the door for her.

She slid inside, rolled down the window so she could hear if Gus called, and reached for the keys—the keys, she suddenly remembered, that were still dangling from the lock to her trunk. "Well, damn."

"Looking for these?"

Grinding her teeth in frustration, she slowly turned toward Nick. Sure enough, there he stood, her keys dangling unrepentantly from his outstretched index finger.

Was she destined to forever look like an idiot in his eyes?

She wiped raindrops from her face, then reached for her keys. "Thank you."

But even with the key and the boost from Gus's industrial strength battery, the old Ford wouldn't start. All it did was whine and crank. Gus got out of his pickup and told her to stop trying. He and Nick leaned over her engine.

Gus stood with the pickup's headlights directly behind him, and Sammi couldn't see his face. But Nick stood at an angle. His sharp, rugged profile stood out starkly against the gloomy evening. His cheekbones appeared even higher than usual, the hollows beneath them deeper. But it was the way the light shot across his moist lips that made Sammi's pulse race.

". . . not getting any fuel."

"Maybe a clogged line."

"Or her fuel pump's gone out."

The men's words brought a sinking feeling to

the pit of her stomach. How expensive was a clogged line? A new fuel pump? They were moot questions. She couldn't afford either. Yet she couldn't be without a car. Her only alternative would be a taxi and she sure couldn't afford that.

"Come on, I'll take you home."

Startled, Sammi looked up to see Nick standing beside her door. Gus joined him. She looked from one man to the other, forlornly. "But—"

"I'll take a look and see what I can do with it when I clock out," Gus said.

"I can't ask you to do that."

"You didn't ask me, I offered. I'll leave a note on your office door to let you know if it's fixed. All you have to do is get yourself home and back again, and Nick's already agreed to see to that. So go, eat a big dinner, put your feet up, and don't worry about your car."

Sammi sighed. She really had no choice but to accept their suggestions. "You know I hate this, don't you?"

Gus waved her words away. "Yeah, yeah. Taking help from friends is a crime, I know. Just give me the keys."

She took her apartment and office keys off the ring and handed Gus the rest. He took them and headed for his truck.

That left Nick. She could either spend money

66

she didn't have on a cab or accept his ride. Meanwhile, he was getting more soaked by the minute. "You're sure you don't mind?"

"I don't mind, as long as you decide before I drown."

Defeated and feeling like a burden, Sammi rolled up her window, grabbed her purse, and got out.

Nick's car was at the other end of the parking lot. They walked quietly side by side across the wet pavement. The rain was picking up again. Her fingers and palm hurt. Her head ached. She'd spent the entire week thus far doing her level best to stay out of Nick's way, and here she was, letting him take her home.

He opened the door of his sleek, bronze Lincoln. She hated to sit on the silky-looking leather upholstery with her damp, rumpled clothes. She hated the thought of confining herself in such a close space with the man who threatened her job, the man who did funny things to her pulse. But just then she was suddenly too tired to worry about any of it.

As she slid onto the seat, the smell of fresh leather teased her. Instead of the loud thunk and rattle she was used to upon slamming her car door, this one closed with a soft, dignified *whap*.

Someday, she promised herself, she would have a new car. Only it wouldn't be a Lincoln. As nice as it was, it wasn't her style. Not that she had a style, but her secret dream had always been a Corvette. Not a newer model, and not a really old classic, but one of the in-betweens. Late seventies, early eighties. She didn't know the exact year, but the look was unforgettable. She would own a metallic-blue Corvette with the body rounded up over the rear wheels. What was that called, anyway? And she wanted one of those scoops on the hood, and a ducktail on the back. And mag wheels. Definitely mag wheels.

Nick opened the driver's door and slid behind the wheel. His car naturally started with barely a twist of the key, then purred like an overfed kitten. No coughing, choking, or clattering from under the hood. Sammi shook her head with disgust.

"Where to?"

His voice came soft and deep and whirled in her mind. She cleared her throat. "On MacArthur, south of Thirty-ninth."

She had to get herself together. These reactions she had to Nick were ridiculous. If she didn't know better, she'd think she was attracted to him. Of course, that wasn't true. And it was just as well, because he certainly couldn't be attracted to her. She was too tall, too plain, too . . . *Okay, let's be honest. You're not woman enough for a man like Nick Elliott.*

If that had been Jim's voice echoing in her head, she would have shoved it aside. But this time it was her own voice, and she knew she spoke the truth.

"Would you like to stop for dinner on the way?"

His words were at such odds with her thoughts, it took her a moment to respond. "Uh, no, thank you."

"You sure? We both have to eat."

"I'll just fix a salad when I get home."

"My treat."

"You don't have to do that."

"You're going to make me eat by myself in a restaurant, then?"

Sammi eyed him carefully. "Is this a sympathy play?"

"Hey." He shrugged. "Whatever works."

Then he did something she wished desperately he hadn't done. Not within her viewing, please. Not when she was tired and her defenses were down. Not when she was sitting next to him in the intimate confines of a rain-shrouded luxury car, only the two of them, alone in the night.

But he did it anyway. He grinned at her.

If she had been standing, her knees would have buckled. Lord have mercy. He had dimples. Cute, boyish dimples, one in each cheek. Heaven help her. "The Village Inn's not too far out of the way."

He didn't ask if she meant to join him, he just grinned wider. "Good."

They rode in silence for several blocks, then Nick flicked on the stereo. His selection of oldies rock surprised her. She would have pegged him more the classical type.

At the restaurant she feigned energy she didn't have and hopped out of the car before he could come around and open her door. When they were inside and seated—a little too close for comfort to a rowdy group of cowboys at a nearby table—Sammi ordered a salad and Nick surprised her again by asking for a chicken fried steak. She'd expected a T-bone.

When the waitress left, Sammi realized how grimy she felt and excused herself. After washing her hands and face and combing her hair in the ladies room, she felt better and returned to the table.

Now she just felt restless. Coming to dinner with Nick hadn't been such a bright idea. What would they possibly talk about? For lack of anything better to do with her hands, she picked up her glass and took a sip of water.

"There's something I've been meaning to ask you," Nick said.

Sammi eyed him warily. "What's that?"

He met her gaze. "If it's none of my business, just say so, but I was wondering . . . just how close are you and Henry?"

Well, she should have known that was coming. Both times Nick had seen her with Henry had surely seemed . . . intimate. First in the hospital, then last Saturday. Now was her opportunity to rid him of his misconceptions.

"Your father and I are close friends."

Nick arched a brow. "Friends?"

"Friends. Close friends, and that's it."

He looked skeptical, but said nothing.

The cowboys two tables away got noisier. By the time the waitress brought Nick's dinner salad, it was obvious to Sammi that the rowdies had spent the better part of the day drinking.

Amid the drone of nearby voices and the clanking of flatware on plates, an uncomfortable silence grew between Nick and Sammi. She couldn't for the life of her think of anything to say to him. She shouldn't have come.

When the waitress finally brought Sammi's salad and Nick's meal, Sammi breathed a sigh of relief. Something to focus her attention on.

"Looks like they're having a good time," Nick said, indicating the cowboys.

"A bunch of drunks," she said with a sneer.

"You disapprove of drinking?"

Sammi washed a bite of salad down with iced tea. "Drinking, no. But those guys are obviously going to drive when they leave here. That, I disapprove of."

"I agree. It's dangerous."

"And plain stupid," she said, heating up to the subject. She knew she should shut her mouth, but the words just poured out. "My husband got behind the wheel when he was

71

drunk. Wrapped himself around a telephone pole."

She felt Nick's close scrutiny. "I didn't know you were married. I assume the accident was serious."

"Fatal."

"I'm sorry."

"Me, too. But not for Jim. It was nobody's fault but his." She gave a wry chuckle. "I only wish if he had to do something so dumb, he'd done it in my Ford instead of his new BMW. And I wish he'd left his mistress at the hotel they'd just checked out of."

Nick gave her a startled look.

Aghast, Sammi dropped her fork and covered her mouth with both palms. "Oh, my God, I'm sorry. I can't believe I said that!" She'd never even told Henry the details of Jim's death. How could she possibly— "I'm sorry."

Nick reached out and took her hands away from her face. "Will you quit apologizing? Chalk it up to a bad day and let it go. Besides," he added with a half-frown, "if the Ford you're talking about is the car you're driving now, I can't but agree with you."

Inappropriate as it was, Sammi broke out laughing and couldn't seem to stop. "I think . . . I'm getting . . . hysterical." She laughed until tears formed. Other diners turned to stare. Slowly, she calmed. "I'm sorry. I don't know what happened."

Nick still held her hands. She tugged them loose.

"Relax," he said. "Your secret's safe with me."

"Oh, it's no secret. At least, it wasn't when it happened. It made all the papers, caused quite a scandal. Seems Jim had been seeing the woman for some time, and she happened to be the wife of one of his partners at the law firm. It's just . . . I guess I've never talked about it before."

"Not even with Henry?"

"No." She shook her head.

"Then I'm glad you felt comfortable enough with me to get it off your chest."

She gave him a wry grin. "I wouldn't exactly say I feel comfortable around you."

He started to take a bite of his chicken fried steak, then stopped. His lips twitched. "Why not?"

"Can we talk about something else?" She picked up her fork and pushed the lettuce around on her plate. The scrape of tines on china made her flinch.

Nick finished the bite he'd interrupted. "I think maybe you and I got off on the wrong foot last week. If you're a significant part of Henry's life—"

"I told you, we're friends. That doesn't constitute a significant part of his life."

"Okay, okay." He raised a hand in defense.

"Maybe you and I could try being friends."

She looked at him skeptically. Who was he trying to kid? Friends? Them?

"Come on, Sammi. Just for tonight. We're not boss and employee until tomorrow morning when we get to work."

She narrowed her gaze. "What is that supposed to mean?"

"Let me rephrase that. How about . . . until I drop you off at your apartment. Friends until then."

She stabbed a cherry tomato with her fork. "Why?"

"Suspicious, aren't you? Okay, never mind. If you'd rather think of me as an ogre with sharp teeth than the nice guy I really am, suit yourself."

"I never said you were an ogre."

"Maybe not, but you act like that's what you think of me."

Sammi popped the cherry tomato into her mouth and chewed it slowly, watching him all the while. Finally she swallowed. "Why do you want to pretend we're friends?"

"I didn't mean pretend. I meant, why don't we try to *be* friends. Why don't we try having a conversation without you getting defensive?"

"Why don't you try dropping my ninety-day probation, friend?" Oh, God. Now she'd done it. She couldn't believe she'd said that.

"See? You must be comfortable around me. Look at all these things you're getting off your chest."

Sammi rolled her eyes.

"To answer your question, I'm not willing to drop the probation. Yet. First I have to be convinced your job is good for the company. But that doesn't mean you have to go out and search for a new job. Even if this one doesn't work out, I wouldn't want you to leave the company."

Sammi looked away quickly, hoping he couldn't see the guilty heat in her cheeks. How had he known she was looking for another place to work?

"When you park in Henry's driveway, you really shouldn't leave the classifieds lying in your front seat. With red circles all over them."

"Oh." Sammi twisted the napkin in her lap. Then she glared at him. "What were you doing snooping around in my car?"

"I wasn't snooping. I had to walk past your car to get to mine. The want ads sort of jumped out at me. When I realized that was your Ford, I was rather hoping you were looking for a replacement for it, not your job. You don't strike me as a quitter."

Sammi's shoulders snapped taut. A quitter? Is that what she was? No. She shook her head. She had spent years backing down from one confrontation after another. She had never even returned defective merchandise to a store for replacement or refund.

No more. If Nick Elliott wanted her to prove herself, she would do it. She would not back down, would not run off to a new job because this one was on shaky ground. "I'm not a quitter."

Nick pursed his lips. "We'll see, won't we?"

Sammi reached for her tea. Her hand shook. Six months ago, even two weeks ago, she would never have had the nerve to even listen to a conversation like this one, let alone take part in it. Maybe that new person she'd been trying to become was finally taking hold. Whatever, she wasn't ready to retreat.

What was it that book on assertiveness said? Something about taking charge rather than being led. She sipped her tea, then set the glass down. "If you want to be friends, I suggest we change the subject."

"Fair enough. Where did you learn to swim so well?"

Sammi grinned. She was going to go home and kiss that book. If there was one thing in the world she didn't mind talking about, it was swimming.

Nick laughed when she told him about her father's lessons, which, when he tossed her into her grandpa's pond that first time, consisted of, "Don't drown, girl."

Next, the conversation turned to travel, which

fascinated Sammi. She'd never been out of the state of Oklahoma. Nick, it seemed, had been all over the world. She listened raptly all through dinner and the drive to her apartment.

She was pleased to notice the rain had stopped.

"You were right," she told him as she reached for the car door handle. "I've enjoyed not being boss and employee. Friends is better. But I've got an ogre with sharp teeth for a boss, and he's supposed to pick me up in the morning, so I better go in."

Nick laughed, then eyed the dark walkway that ran through the apartment buildings. His smile disappeared. "This place could use a few dozen security lights. I'll take you to your door."

"You don't have to do that."

"Yes, I do. A man friend doesn't let a woman friend walk alone in places like this. We pay you enough. You should be living someplace safer than this. For that matter, you should also be driving a better car. What do you do with that outrageous salary of yours, bet on the horses?"

She couldn't take offense at his words, not the way he was smiling. "Remember that BMW I told you about?"

"Yeah."

"It wasn't paid for."

"So? The insurance should have taken care of

77

it."

"That wasn't paid for, either. Let's drop it. My finances aren't your problem."

"True enough." Nick opened his door and looked back at her. "I do my part—I sign the paychecks."

"Braggart."

He walked her to her apartment door, staying so close to her that his shoulder occasionally brushed hers. The intimacy the slight touch suggested made her fingers forget how to turn the key in the lock. Finally she got the door open and turned to say good night.

"Are we still friends?" Nick asked.

Something in his eyes, his voice, made her breath catch. She cleared her throat. "Until you drop me off at my apartment, and here I am."

Nick took her by the shoulders and pulled her closer to him, his face suddenly serious. "You're not in your apartment yet, so I'm not your boss, you're not my employee. Right?"

She tried to read his expression. *Intense* was the only word that came to mind. Her heart gave a sharp thud. "I—"

"Right?"

"I guess."

"Good." He leaned closer and bent his head down.

Oh good Lord, he was going to kiss her. And heaven help her, she was going to let him.

"Nick—"

"Sammi." He smiled. "It's just a kiss between friends. Just a kiss."

But it wasn't. When his lips brushed hers with a light, teasing motion, Sammi lost her breath. Then his mouth returned, once, twice. His arms wrapped around her back and pressed her lightly against his chest. She braced her hands there and found it broader than it looked, harder, yet not flat. Ridges and mounds of muscles fascinated her palms. She couldn't believe this was happening.

His lips lingered, the kiss deepened. When she opened her mouth, his tongue met hers. She tasted the peppermint he'd sucked on after dinner.

Heat suffused her and emotions swelled. His lips were firm and silky against hers. She couldn't get enough of them, enough of him. Lord, what was happening to her? The world was spinning and she couldn't seem to stop it, didn't want to try.

He gripped her tighter in his arms. Her hands were trapped between their bodies. She didn't care, so long as he kept kissing her. All she could think as her knees turned to water, was *Yes . . . oh, yes*.

Her breath rasped in her throat. Her fingers pressed harder into the muscled wall of his chest.

And then he was taking his mouth away.

"No," she whispered. And he came back, first with a slow flick of his tongue on her mole. The blatantly erotic gesture wrung a moan from her. Then he took her mouth again, fiercely this time, taking everything she offered. And giving. Giving more than she'd ever dreamed a man could give with a kiss.

With one hand he cradled her head. Instead of feeling threatening, his grip felt good. Right. Necessary.

A teenage giggle from down the sidewalk brought the world snapping back into place. What was the matter with her? Had she lost her mind? What was she doing kissing Nick Elliott?

She pulled abruptly away from his mouth and gasped to catch her breath. Then gasped again. His eyes, bright, laughing blue only moments ago, now glittered as black as a pair of onyx stones. He, too, had trouble catching his breath.

Sammi couldn't blame him, even in her own mind, for what had just happened. She had wanted it, taken it, reveled in it. For that, she could only blame herself. "What are we doing?" she whispered.

He searched her face intently, looking for what, she couldn't guess. The same long finger that had earlier dangled her keys in the parking lot now stroked her cheek, her lips.

"Just saying good night, Sammi. Just saying

good night."

She swallowed. "I've ... done smarter things."

He gave her a wry grin. "So have I. Now go inside and lock your door. I'll pick you up at seven-thirty in the morning."

"That's all right. I'll call a cab."

"Call one if you like." He shrugged and turned her loose. "But I'll still be here at seven-thirty."

All Sammi could do was nod. It was surprising how hard a body could tremble and still remain upright. She looked at him one more time, still stunned by what had just happened, then stepped into her apartment and locked the door.

The echo of his footsteps down the sidewalk taunted her. Fool! reverberated in her mind with every step he took.

Never in her life had she been kissed like that. Never had she felt such overwhelming physical and emotional responses. Heaven help her, was she falling for the man?

Tears, swift and hot, stung the backs of her eyes. What had meant the world to her had meant little or nothing to him beyond the moment. He'd said so himself. *Just saying good night, Sammi. Just saying good night.*

Doubt dogged Nick's every step as he took

the dark walkway back to his car. Just saying good night.

Hell. It felt a damn sight more like hello to him.

He'd played the game and taken her mind off her troubles for a while, loosened her up a bit. He hadn't meant to kiss her, had no idea why he'd done it.

Liar.

Okay, so he'd been wanting to kiss her for days. He still had no business doing it.

The problem now was, now that he'd tasted her, how the hell was he going to keep from doing it again?

Five

At ten o'clock the next morning Nick felt unaccountably nervous. He couldn't remember the last time he'd felt uncomfortable about his behavior with a woman. He shouldn't be feeling so now. All he'd done was kiss her.

Kiss her until your hands shook, you mean.

Okay, so it was more than a kiss. So she was his employee, and therefore off-limits. It wasn't as if he had asked her to marry him. He didn't know why he was so worked up.

Sammi certainly didn't seem upset. She seemed to have recovered just fine by the time he'd picked her up this morning. She'd been quiet on the way to work, but she hadn't seemed nervous. Hadn't given the least indication that she wanted it to happen again. That it had happened at all.

So why the hell hadn't she shown up for the staff meeting an hour ago?

Maybe she wasn't so calm after all. Maybe she just hid behind that aloof expression of

83

hers. Or maybe she wasn't worried about missing the meeting because she was too busy looking for another job. Whatever her reasons, he intended to find out.

He picked up the phone. There was no answer on Sammi's extension. He dialed his secretary. "Marie, see if you can track down Sammi. Tell her I need to see her in my office right away."

Sammi was gathering evaluation comments from production workers on the new Video Jet paint marker when word filtered down that she was being summoned to Nick's office. Great. She had hoped to avoid him for a little longer. At least until she could forget the way he'd held and kissed her last night.

But no, he wasn't going to give her time for that. Why should he? As far as he was concerned, it meant nothing. That was exactly how she had forced herself to act this morning, too, and how she would have to act from now on. As though the kiss meant nothing. As though his touch hadn't burned her, his lips hadn't seared her soul.

She crossed from the paint building into the broiling sun, then through Processing and Staging before she finally reached the air-conditioned offices. Just what she needed to appear calm — sweat running down her temples. She pulled off her safety glasses and dodged into the ladies room, disgusted to find her hands shaking.

After washing them in blessedly cool water, she dabbed at her face with a damp paper towel. She had to appear unfazed, under control.

Several deep breaths later she stepped out into the hall and headed for Nick's office.

"There you are," Marie said. "Nick's been looking for you."

"So I heard. What's up?"

Marie shrugged. "I have no idea."

With her stomach in a knot — oh, how she did not want to face him — she entered his office.

Nick breathed a sigh of relief. He'd almost begun to think she'd completely disappeared. It had been an hour since he'd asked Marie to find her. A long, frustrating sixty minutes.

He got up from his desk and closed his office door. "Where have you been?"

She arched a brow. "Working."

"Why weren't you at the meeting this morning?"

"What meeting?"

Nick forcibly unclenched his jaw and returned to stand beside his desk. "The staff meeting I sent you a memo about first thing today."

She looked surprised. "I didn't get one."

"How would you know? You haven't been in your office all day."

"Now wait—"

"No, you wait." He crossed the room until he stood before her. She backed away a step, her eyes wide. Good. She wasn't as sure of herself—or him—as he'd thought. She deserved to be a little nervous after the morning he'd had.

He, Nick Elliott, who had been so careful all his adult life to avoid any and all sticky situations with people he worked with, suddenly found himself knee-deep in the very mire he'd always sidestepped.

"No," he repeated, "you wait. This is about last night, isn't it?"

"I don't know what you're talking about."

"Sure you do. Last night? At your apartment door? Your lips, my li—"

"I get the picture. But what does that have to do with my not getting a memo about a meeting?"

Nick paused. "You really didn't get it?"

"Of course not. Otherwise I would have been there."

He studied her closely. There was more going on inside her head than she was telling, but he had a feeling she meant it about the memo. In which case, he'd just made an ass of himself.

"I'm sorry. I thought . . ." He heaved a sigh

86

and looked at the ceiling. "I thought maybe you skipped the meeting because of last night." He looked at her, but now she stood at the window with her back to him.

"You did?"

He let out a self-deprecating chuckle. "Pretty stupid of me, wasn't it? But then last night wasn't real smart, either. Look, Sammi, I started that business and I shouldn't have. I apologize. I don't want you going around worrying that I'm going to accost you in the hall or something. Last night . . . well, it won't happen again, believe me."

Sammi held her breath and closed her eyes on the view of the Wiley Post Airport runway outside the window. Sharp pain knifed somewhere in the region of her heart. If she'd had any doubts about how Nick felt about kissing her, she didn't now.

"Fine." She turned back to face him. "What did I miss at the meeting?"

Stung by her coolness, the look of haughty disdain on her face, Nick strode back to his desk. He wished he could dismiss that ground-shaking kiss as easily as she apparently had. "We talked about current projects. I'd like to hear about yours, but I have another appointment in five minutes. We'll talk tomorrow." He checked his calendar. "At two-thirty. And I'll need your budget proposal for next year by the end of the week. Give it to Marie as soon as it's ready."

"Anything else?"

Yeah, he thought. *I'd like to wipe that icy look off your face, lady. I'd like to melt it away with—* Good God. He was actually contemplating kissing her again. "No."

Sammi flinched at his harsh tone.

Hell. Now she had him shouting at her. He cleared his throat and tried for calm. "No, that's all for now."

"Fine." She started for the door. "I'll see you tomorrow at two-thirty."

By the time her footsteps faded down the hall, Nick almost had control over the urge to throw something.

Sammi walked straight from Nick's office to hers. Walked, when she wanted nothing more than to run. Gnawed on her lips when she wanted to scream.

"Hey, Sammi, I fi—"

She cut Gus off with a curt, "I'll talk to you later." If she had to be civil to anyone right now she would choke on it.

How could he! How could Nick so easily dismiss what had happened between them?

She slammed her office door, not caring who heard, and leaned back against it. With her eyes squeezed shut, she took huge breaths, one after the other, but the shaking deep inside her wouldn't stop.

That *man*. First he threatened her job, now he threatened her sanity.

I told you, Sammi, you just don't have what a man needs.

She pressed her hands against her temples and silently screamed at the voice in her head — Jim's voice, her voice — to go away. She knew she wasn't the type who attracted men. She knew that. But Nick had kissed her, damn it. He had started it.

Yes, and he had finished it. *Just a good-night kiss between friends*. He had walked away, when she'd barely been able to stand.

And then he had ruined it. *Stupid . . . shouldn't have . . . won't happen again*.

Damn him.

She pushed away from the door and sank onto her chair. "I'm a bigger idiot than I thought."

How could she have imagined things would turn out any other way? How could she even have hoped Nick would want to kiss her again?

She couldn't have, shouldn't have. She knew better.

The one thing she couldn't get straight in her mind, though, was why he had kissed her in the first place. Yet even that didn't matter. He'd made it plain he wanted nothing more to do with her, personally speaking. In a few weeks, that might extend to their working relationship, too, unless she could convince him otherwise. To do that, she had to show him how professional she was, how much she could contribute to Elliott Air.

And she couldn't do either by missing staff meetings. With determination, she picked up the phone and called Marie. But Marie swore she had placed the memo on Sammi's desk that morning, along with the latest copy of *Business & Commercial Aviation*.

Sammi thanked Marie and hung up. Neither the memo nor the magazine were on her desk. Terrific. How was she supposed to convince Nick of her professionalism if she couldn't even keep track of her paperwork?

She found the missing items five minutes later in the bottom of her wastebasket, underneath the empty orange juice can and donut wrapper she had thrown away that morning. She distinctly remembered throwing those things into an empty wastebasket.

Then again, maybe . . . maybe she was losing her mind.

Later that afternoon Sammi was still trying to figure out how her memo and magazine had ended up in the trash, when the answer came to her.

As she worked on her secret project, the one she hadn't even told Henry about, she spread magazine clippings and historical reports across her desk until she ran out of space. Her phone rang. When she answered it, the cord dragged across the papers and nudged a set of fifteen-year-old production figures over the edge and into the wastebasket.

End of mystery.

And no wonder it had happened. Her desk nearly filled her tiny office, but the top was still awfully small.

"I can't work like this."

"What was that?" Marie asked over the phone.

Sammi told Marie what had just happened. "Any chance of me getting into the conference room for a couple of hours this afternoon? I need table space—desperately."

"Sure," Marie said. "It's free and clear. I'll put you down on the schedule. You can go any time. And speaking of time, I called to make sure I've got your appointment for tomorrow correct. You're seeing Nick at two-thirty?"

The reminder made Sammi grit her teeth. "Right."

"Got it. Have fun in the conference room."

Sammi hung up the phone and grinned. She

would have fun in the conference room. Her special project was the most exciting, most ambitious thing she had ever tackled. If she could put together a convincing enough proposal, it was going to—what was it Henry always said?— knock the socks off not only Nick, Henry, and Elliott Air but the entire aircraft industry, too.

To heck with finding another job before she lost this one. She still had some time. She couldn't, for the life of her, bring herself to walk out on this project. She was going to put Elliott Air on the map, in the news, and in the history books. Or she was going to go down trying.

Within ten minutes she had all her materials spread out across the huge conference table and was mentally buried in reports, ideas, and excitement. For luck, she raised an imaginary toast to the picture on the wall across from her.

Goose bumps ran down her arms. There was something . . . emotional, something thrilling in the shot of a brand new Elliott Skybird 2000 rolling out of the hangar for the first time, paint so fresh and gleaming she swore she could smell it every time she looked at the enlarged photo.

How she would have loved to have worked here ten years ago when the Skybirds had been in production. She could imagine herself standing in the yard watching the ultimate in owner-flown planes taxiing toward the runway. The single engine craft was known for its turbo-charged speed and pressurized comfort, its reliability and safety.

The 2000s still in the air were the best piston engine planes in existence. Just thinking about the financial difficulties that forced Elliott Air to stop producing the plane made her want to cry.

But Elliott Air hadn't been the only company crippled by unfair lawsuits. How the courts could award multimillion dollar judgments to the widows of careless pilots, weekend aces who did asinine things like run out of fuel, was beyond Sammi's understanding. Yet it had happened, over and over again. It didn't seem to matter that a crash in question was caused by pilot error. Survivors were legally allowed to sue anyone and everyone involved in the manufacture and sale of the aircraft.

Even Elliott's suppliers had been hit hard, so much so many of them had stopped producing parts for private, owner-flown planes altogether. No one was safe.

Sammi had read of more than one instance of pilot error in which the courts held judgment against a gasket manufacturer, when the gasket had nothing to do with the crash.

It wasn't right, damn it.

Sammi gripped her pen until her knuckles

ached. It wasn't fair that Elliott and other companies like them had to stop building planes because of a lawsuit-happy society. How could anyone think an aircraft manufacturer could shell out a couple of million dollars a whack and still stay in business, when the plane in question only sold for sixty thousand?

The companies who built aircraft for corporate use weren't as affected by lawsuits as were those who built private planes. Corporate aircraft were normally flown by professional pilots who had proper training. Pilots who, as a rule, did not run out of fuel through carelessness; did not overload their planes with too many people, too much baggage; did not get themselves lost or fly into mountains or any other of the dozens of things weekend aces seemed to do with startling regularity.

Granted, not all private pilots were guilty of such negligence—most were careful and conscientious. But far too many ended up in fatal accidents.

Voices from the hall tried to distract her, but Sammi ignored them and stared at the picture on the wall. Gradually it calmed her, and the excitement came rushing back. Then the door behind her flew open.

"A little hanky-panky with the new boss, and you don't have time for us little people anymore, is that it?"

Sammi whirled toward the sarcastic voice. "Gus! Wha—"

He tossed a set of keys to her—her keys. She barely caught them. "Your car's fixed, Ms Carmichael."

"Oh. Gus, thank you. That's what you were trying to tell me earlier when I cut you off. I'm sorry. That was incredibly rude of me. I just . . . I had a lot on my mind."

"No kidding." His lip curled. "Walking out of the boss's office with your eyes glassy and your mouth all red and swollen, I can just imagine what you had on your mind."

Sammi could only stare at him, stunned. She touched her lips, remembering how she had bit them to keep from screaming in frustration.

"We all knew you and Henry were just good friends. But with Nick, hell, Sammi, nobody's going to buy it. You watch yourself. There's already talk."

Without waiting for a reply, Gus stomped down the hall. While she stared, stunned, at the empty doorway, Nick appeared.

"Why did you let him get away with that?"

"I . . ." She threw a hand in the air, not sure what to say. Then she noticed his expression. He was angry. Her neck and shoulders stiffened. "Don't worry, I'll straighten him out. Your reputation will be quite safe."

Then she turned back toward the table, hoping he'd leave her alone.

He didn't. He approached the table and stood beside her, scanning the material she had spread out. "What are you doing in here?"

"I needed the space. Marie said the room was available."

"What are you working on?"

She picked up her pen and leaned over her legal pad. "Just a project." Why didn't he go away?

"What kind of project?"

"It's . . ." She craned her neck to look up at him. "It's too soon to talk about it. I haven't finished my research yet."

She watched with a sinking feeling as Nick picked up one set of historical records after another, his brow furrowing deeper by the minute.

Then he picked up the one item that, if he was as smart as she thought he was, would tell him what she was up to. He read the copy of the Product Liability Bill currently in Congress. The bill that, if passed, would limit the amount for which a company could be held liable and allow companies like Elliott to resume production of personal aircraft at a much more reasonable risk.

He looked at the paper so long he must have read every word, when the first couple of sentences would have told him all he needed to know. Her palms broke out in sweat.

96

His chest rose and fell. Sharply. Twice. When he jerked his head up, he glanced first at the photo on the wall, the one she had been studying, then he met her gaze.

Sammi sucked in a breath. The blatant excitement, the undeniable longing she saw in his eyes sent a spiral of hope curling through her chest. Then caution crossed his face.

"Is this . . ." He motioned toward the papers in his hand and those on the table. "Is this what I think it is? Are you about to propose we start building planes again?"

Her neck ached from looking up at him. She stood and walked to the end of the table. "I'm not ready to propose anything yet. I'm just investigating."

"Sammi, we can't—"

"Don't tell me to stop, Nick. I saw that look on your face. You're just like Henry, aren't you? You'd give your right eye to be able to build planes again."

For a moment he closed his eyes, then looked at the picture on the wall again. "It doesn't matter." He turned away and tossed the copy of the Product Liability Bill onto the table. "It doesn't matter who wants what. We stopped building planes because we damn near lost the company."

"But if this new bill passes—"

"If this new bill passes, within twenty-four

hours you'll see at least a dozen dead companies spring back to life and start building small aircraft."

"And not one of them as good as the Skybird 2000."

Nick let out a short breath, then flashed his dimples. "You've got me there."

Doing her best to ignore what those dimples did to her heart rate, Sammi decided it was time to push the issue of building planes.

"Just think about it, Nick." Urgency drove her forward until she stood right before him and grasped him by his upper arms. "Imagine standing out there watching a brand new Skybird 2000 roll out of that hangar. Maybe even a 3000, if we wanted. *Imagine it,* Nick!"

Nick could see it. Easily. He'd wanted it often enough during the past ten years. He had grown up watching his father's planes roll out of that last hangar. Seeing a plane he'd helped build with his own two hands, his own sweat and effort—just remembering it, anticipating it, sent chills up his spine.

Yes, he wanted to see the 2000 in production again. But when he dreamed, another aircraft, bigger, faster than the 2000, appeared in his vision. Built for corporate rather than personal use.

And he had almost had it. He had designed one himself from wing tip to wing tip, nose to tail. He had labored and sweated through the rigid FAA testing.

And he lost it, simply by having faith in a man he should have known better than to trust. For once in his life Nick should have listened to Henry, who'd warned him more than once not to believe Sam Barnett's words.

But before the bottom fell out and Nick lost everything he worked for, he had been on top of the world. There was no other feeling like designing, building and testing his own plane. Nothing in the world . . .

Except perhaps, he thought, the feeling of Sammi's hands on his coat sleeves. The heat, the sheer power that filled him at her touch made him tremble.

Look at her. Her face glowed with excitement, her brown eyes sparkled gold and green. Sheer energy vibrated from her to him. God, she was magnificent!

Without thinking, he gripped her bent elbows and pulled her closer. Like a compass needle pointing north, he was attracted to her. She called him, drew him. If she did it deliberately, she was damned good at it. Right then he didn't care. It was wrong, it was stupid, it was dangerous. But he was going to go back on his word. He was going to kiss her. And by the look in her eyes, she was going to let him.

Let him, hell. That look was an open invitation if he'd ever seen one. And he'd seen more than a few. "Sammi?"

"Yes," came her throaty answer.

His heart thumped harder. He gripped her elbows tighter, pulling her closer and bending his head. She raised hers.

"Oh! Excuse me."

The feminine voice from the doorway echoed like a shot going off in the dead of night. Nick and Sammi jerked apart as though stung. He whirled around in time to see Darla Grayson, the Operations secretary, back away from the door.

"Damn." How could he have been so careless? He'd promised Sammi it wouldn't happen again. Not only had he nearly broken his word, he'd done so at work, in a place where anyone could—and did—walk by.

What was it about Sammi Carmichael that made him lose all his sense? He ran a shaking hand through his hair and slowly turned back to face her.

"So." She cleared her throat and sat down. "I'd better get back to work."

She could go back to work, while he was standing there with his brains scrambled and his pulse pounding? Her sudden coolness, after the fire she'd unleashed in him, made him grind his teeth. "You're wasting your time on this project."

"You don't mean that."

She looked like he'd just stolen her favorite toy. To hell with the little tease. "I do mean it. That bill could pass tomorrow and it wouldn't make any difference to Elliott Air's current operation. In case you haven't noticed, Ms Executive, there's a recession going on. We don't have the money to retool, and with this lousy economy, we'd never be able to borrow enough. It's a waste of time."

"Nick, I'm not asking for anything but the opportunity to investigate the idea. It's my job. It's what you pay me for, what Henry paid me for."

He glared at her. She sat there so calm and cool, looking up at him with her hair in that tight little knot. But her eyes still flashed with heat and her lips still called to his. Damn her.

"What else was Henry paying you for?"

Six

Nick couldn't believe he'd said that to Sammi. All night long his own vicious words echoed in his ears. After he got to the office the next morning he still couldn't believe it. There was only one explanation for what he'd said to her in the conference room before walking out and leaving her pale and shaking. The reason for all his bizarre behavior and thoughts was that Sammi Carmichael was swiftly and surely driving him stark raving nuts.

He tossed that morning's business section from the paper onto his desk. He'd been trying to read it for ten minutes, but couldn't concentrate worth a damn. Truth was, he wouldn't be able to concentrate on anything until he cleared the air with Sammi and apologized, for the second time in two days.

Calling Sammi's office would, he knew, be a waste of time. If there was one thing he'd

102

learned about her in recent days, it was that the lady never sat still. She was all over the plant constantly. He reached for the phone, thinking to have Marie find her and ask her to come to see him.

He put the phone down. After what he'd said to Sammi yesterday, she would probably ignore his request to come to his office, so he would go to hers.

But she likely wouldn't be there.

If she's not there, I'll wait for her.

The thought of being enclosed in that former broom closet of hers made sweat pop out along his forehead. No, he couldn't talk to her there, not in a place so damn small. He didn't trust himself around a woman who affected him the way she did. And he couldn't talk to her down in the plant where the machinery noise would force him to yell to be heard, where a hundred pairs of eyes would watch every move he made.

His office it would have to be. He picked up the phone again, then once more put it down. She was scheduled to meet with him at two-thirty. He would apologize, and apologize sincerely, this afternoon. And he would keep his damn hands and his petty insults to himself.

Sammi spent the day just as she had spent every minute since Nick had walked out of the conference room yesterday—vacillating between righteous fire-breathing rage and sickening, gut-wrenching distress. Even the tears she'd soaked her pillow with during the night had been both angry and miserable.

Now she had to go to his office and face him across that smooth mahogany desk for their two-thirty appointment. Her emotions were still so close to the surface, she feared if he even looked at her crossways she would either scream or burst into tears. How could she let the man get to her the way he did?

That's easy, Sammi, you're an idiot.

This time it was her own voice sounding in her head, and she agreed with it wholeheartedly. In her juvenile enthusiasm over the Skybird 2000 she had practically thrown herself at Nick. True, he had almost kissed her, but then Nick didn't seem like a man who would turn down a woman begging to be kissed.

But what if . . . *Oh, my word.* What if he really had wanted to kiss her? What if he felt even a tenth of the heat that flared in her veins at the thought of him? He would have kissed her if Darla hadn't walked by.

She could drive herself crazy with what-ifs.

The lesson she was learning from all this was how devastating, how totally distracting a fierce attraction to a certain man could be. What she had felt for Jim when they had married, what she had thought at the time was wild passion and everlasting love, seemed tepid compared to the way she felt about Nick Elliott. Her *boss,* for crying out loud.

"It won't do, Sammi," she told herself. She picked up the files on her current projects and lectured herself all the way to Nick's office. She would be courteous, professional, and cool. Assertive, yet polite. She would not make a fool out of herself. Not again.

But then, after that crack of his yesterday about what Henry was paying her for, rather than yearning for a kiss, she might just as easily sock Nick Elliott a good one right in the mouth.

"Go right on in," Marie told her.

Yep. Right in the ol' kisser. The thought made her grin. She was still grinning when she walked into Nick's office. He was apparently surprised by her mood. Good. It was time he was off balance for a change. "Good afternoon," she said. "Would you like the door open or closed?"

He eyed her carefully. "Closed," he said finally.

Sammi kept the picture firmly in mind of her fist connecting with his face and nearly laughed out loud.

"You're certainly in a good mood. After yesterday I wouldn't blame you if you came in here swinging."

Startled, she almost tripped. She glared at

him. How dare he read her so easily. "The thought of punching you a good one did cross my mind a time or two." She sat on the chair in front of his desk.

"Look, Sammi." Nick glanced toward the window and ran a hand through his hair. "I was way out of line yesterday. What I said, about you and Henry . . . I don't know why I even said it. Even if it were true, it wouldn't be any of my business." He looked at her then, yet she couldn't read his expression. "But I know it's not true. Anyone can take one look at you and know you're nobody's kept woman."

God, it hurt! She knew men weren't attracted to her. She was too tall, too shy. Her hair was too red and she had a mole on her face. But God, to have Nick come right out and say she wasn't even attractive enough to be some man's mistress!

I told you, Sammi, you just don't have what a man needs.

Jim's voice whispering in her mind was like a kick in the chest. She squeezed her eyes shut and clenched her jaw against the pain. Nick's affirmation of what she already knew about herself was like having a rug yanked out from under her.

"Sammi?"

She wanted to scream at him. She wanted to cry. She did neither, just slowly opened her eyes and stared at the files in her lap.

"I'm sorry, Sammi. I know that doesn't make up for what I did and said yesterday, but I am sorry."

Sammi cleared her throat and raised her gaze as far as the edge of his desk. "I'm sure you have other business this afternoon, so I won't take long." She picked up three of the folders from her lap. "You already know about the Elf Inventory Control system, the nesting program, and the computerized router."

She placed the backup information on his desk, then picked up another folder.

Nick leaned forward in his chair and ignored the files. "Tell me about this Elf system. How does it work?"

Damn him, he knew exactly how the system worked. "A little green guy with big pointy ears runs around and keeps track of where everything is," she told him.

Nick's mouth tightened as he arched a brow, but he said nothing.

Sammi took a deep breath. "All right. Computer terminals containing all the part numbers are placed in every section downstairs. Whenever a part is moved from one location to another, the person doing the moving stops at the terminal before leaving the area and runs the electronic wand over the control sheet that accompanies the parts. That way the system knows the parts are leaving the area. When they reach their destination, they're checked into the

107

new location the same way. The location of any part can be checked on the computer any time, so we always know where everything is."

Nick still sat there with that eyebrow cocked, and didn't say a word.

Sammi crossed her arms and glared at him. "Satisfied?"

Without commenting on the Elf at all, he pulled the files toward him. "What else do you have?"

Sammi felt like grinding her teeth. Instead, she held up the file in her hand. "This is the information on the Video Jet paint marker we installed last year."

"What does it mark?" The leather of his chair creaked as he leaned back.

"It numbers all the parts we manufacture. The operator punches in the part number, serial number, whatever else a particular set of parts requires, on a keypad. A conveyor belt carries each part beneath an electronic eye. When the eye detects the part, it sprays the information onto it."

"We're too fancy these days to use a rubber stamp?"

Sammi raised her gaze and glared at him. He might tell her to her face her job was unnecessary and that she was too unattractive for a man to want, but he better not belittle her machines, damn it. "We're too good a company to send out parts with smeared numbers nobody can read. This way we do it right the first time, and don't have to redo it."

"This jet sprayer does a good job, then?"

"It does an excellent job."

"What happens when someone keys in the wrong information? Does that set of parts go out bearing two sets of numbers, if we're lucky enough to catch the mistake?"

Her shoulder muscles were getting tighter by the minute. "Our people are very careful. If a mistake should happen, which it hasn't, we can black out the incorrect information and redo the numbering."

She tossed the Video Jet file onto his desk and picked up the next one. "Those projects you have on your desk are completed. The equipment is up and running, and I monitor all of it regularly."

He nodded toward the file in her hand. "What's the last one?"

Call her job unimportant, will he? He wouldn't be able to resist what she held in her hand. "This is my current project. I want to have a company come here and demonstrate their Theodolite System. It's an optic system, computer operated, that makes the way we master fixtures obsolete."

Look at him sit up in his chair. She had him now. "If what I've read is true, this system will do in less than a day what now takes us four or five days. Our shifts won't have to spend their holidays mastering Interchangeability Control Points, and we won't have to pay them double and triple time for doing it."

He leaned back in his chair again. "Have you set up the demo yet?"

The sorry so-and-so wasn't going to give her an inch. But no matter how disinterested he acted, she knew better. He was too good a businessman—or, as Henry's son, he should be—to miss the significance of increased production, reduced downtime, less overtime, and employees who got holidays off.

"Before I call them," she said, "I want to make sure you'll be available when they come."

He raised a brow. "For this, I'll be available. Get with Marie. She has my schedule."

Ahh, Sammi thought. Sweet satisfaction. He liked the sound of her project. There was no way he could deny it. She placed the Theodolite file on his desk and started to rise.

Nick's phone rang. He answered it, then said, "Hold on, Henry." With his hand over the mouthpiece, he asked Sammi to wait.

She didn't want to wait, but she had his attention on her current project. Now was not the time to alienate him.

"Of course I remember where you live," Nick said into the phone. "Did you forget you're retired? . . . I can't tonight, I've got too much work. . . . Sorry, but I could have sworn the new letterhead listed me as president."

Sammi winced at his sarcastic tone. Henry was probably asking for the latest details of the business.

"I said — no. At seven o'clock tonight I'll be hip-deep in paperwork. I won't have time for dinner. We'll talk later. Maybe tomorrow." Without waiting for a reply, Nick hung up.

He gave Sammi a wry look. "What do you do with a former company president who won't let go?"

So far in the past week, he had attacked her job, her morals, her looks, her projects. Now he was maligning Henry. As far as Sammi was concerned, Nick Elliott had just gone too far.

"That former company president, as you so impersonally put it, happens to be your father. He's lonely, he's feeling left out of things, and he's just had a heart attack."

"From which he recovered nicely."

What a jerk! She sauntered toward his desk. "Let's do a repeat of the other night — for a minute, let's just be friends instead of boss and employee. As your non-employee, I'd like to say you have to be the most insensitive, unfeeling, coldhearted louse I've ever met. I know you and Henry don't get along very well —"

"That's an understatement."

"But for crying out loud, the man is your father. That heart attack could have killed him. Don't you even care?"

Nick's jaw hardened with every word she

111

spoke. "Even for a, what did you call yourself, a friend, a non-employee? My relationship with Henry is none of your business. Just stay out of it, Carmichael."

"My business or not—" She braced her knuckles on the edge of his desk and leaned over. "—your relationship with Henry stinks, Elliott. He's just handed you an entire company, a good one, on a silver platter. The least you could do is show a little gratitude." With that, Sammi whirled around and stormed out of the office.

What a total ass that man was! If he dealt with clients the way he dealt with her and Henry, it was no wonder Elliott Air had been forced to stop building aircraft. Nick probably ran off all the potential buyers, the jerk.

Just because Nick was a sorry S.O.B. didn't mean Henry should have to be alone when he wanted company. If his own son wouldn't take time for a visit, Sammi would. Henry was obviously lonely or he'd never have bothered calling Nick.

At seven that evening, the time she'd heard Nick mention on the phone, she hid her small bouquet behind her back and rang Henry's doorbell.

Even with her new executive salary, the daisies and baby's breath were an extravagance she could barely afford. But if they lightened Henry's mood, made him feel less alone, showed him that someone cared, then they were worth every penny.

She took a deep breath to relax. Whatever happened, she didn't want her anger with Nick to show. She didn't even want Henry to know she was aware of his dinner invitation to Nick.

Finally the door opened.

Sammi held the bouquet before her face. "Surprise! Mind if I come in?"

"That depends. Who are you?"

Shock and confusion held Sammi motionless behind her flowers. That soft feminine voice did not belong to Henry! Nor did it sound at all like Mrs. Simms.

"Henry, I believe you have a guest," the woman said.

A gust of wind blew a baby's breath blossom directly up Sammi's nose. She jerked the flowers away and sneezed.

"Bless you," the stranger said.

"Sammi?" Henry's voice, thank heaven.

With heat creeping up her cheeks, Sammi opened her eyes. She halfway smiled. "Hi, Henry."

The lady beside him radiated confidence and grace the way a turned-on bulb sent out light. Her perfectly-coifed ash-blond head reached just to the top of Henry's shoulder. Everything about her, from the diamonds at her ears and throat to the raw-silk jumpsuit she wore spoke of wealth, but in an understated way. She was unquestionably beautiful.

"This is a surprise," Henry said. "I wasn't expecting you."

"I . . . can see that." What to do? How to get out of this gracefully? "I just thought I'd drop these flowers off on my way home."

"Nonsense." Henry pushed open the storm door. "You can't just whiz by like that. Come in, come in." He took Sammi by the arm and pulled her into the house.

"I don't want to interrupt your evening," she said.

"Don't be silly." He turned to the woman at his side. "Ernestine, I'd like you to meet Samantha Carmichael. Sammi is the Director of Advanced Technology at Elliott Air, as well as a good friend. Sammi, this is Ernestine Winfield, my . . . another dear friend of mine."

Winfield. The name, along with the face, clicked into place like two perfectly matched cogs. Ernestine Winfield was the widow of John Winfield, founder of Winfield Oil and Exploration. According to the papers, she still owned the controlling share of stock, although her brother-in-law now ran the company.

Mrs. Winfield was also a prominent socialite, actively involved in the annual Beaux Arts Ball and other fund-raising activities around the city and state, and surprisingly, she was an influential women's rights activist.

"Nice to meet you," Sammi said.

Mrs. Winfield held out her hand to shake. "The pleasure is mine, and you're not interrupting a thing, I promise."

Her handshake was firm and friendly, her smile genuine. Sammi liked her instantly.

"Of course you're not interrupting anything." Henry ushered the two women into the living room. "Ernestine and I were just having a cocktail before dinner. You'll stay, won't you, Sammi?"

"Oh, I couldn't, Henry."

"Of course you can. Mrs. Simms made lasagna, so there's plenty of food. Can I get you a drink?"

Sammi declined. She felt like a fifth wheel.

"Are those for me?" Henry asked.

Sammi looked down at the daisies in her hand. She'd forgotten them. "I thought they might cheer you up." She grinned. "But I see they weren't necessary."

Henry took the bouquet. "They are cheery, aren't they? I'll put them in a vase."

"I'll help you," Sammi offered.

"No, no. You two girls have a seat and get to know each other. I'll be right back."

If Sammi could have dug a hole in the floor, she would have crawled into it and pulled the carpet over her head. How embarrassing to interrupt their private, obviously intimate dinner. What in the world was she going to say to a woman like Ernestine Winfield?

115

* * *

Nick leaned back in his chair and rubbed his eyes in frustration. How the hell was he supposed to get any work done when Sammi's parting words kept ringing in his ears?

Insensitive, unfeeling, coldhearted louse . . .

He's lonely, he's feeling left out of things and he's just had a heart attack. That heart attack could have killed him. Don't you even care?

As rocky as his and Henry's relationship had been for more than twenty years, Nick acknowledged that he did care. Why, he couldn't imagine. In all those twenty-some years, Henry had never given him a reason to.

Maybe it was the years before—Nick's growing-up years when he and Henry had been more than father and son, when they had been buddies. Maybe it was those memories that wouldn't allow Nick to completely let go.

Whatever, between his own feelings and Sammi's words, his concentration was shot. Guilt over his treatment of Henry on the phone nagged at him. What would it hurt to stop by the house for a few minutes? He didn't have to stay for dinner.

With his mind made up, he shoved back from his desk and rolled down his shirt-sleeves. Sammi was right. It must have been hard for Henry to step down from the presidency of Elliott Air, a company he founded before Nick was born, and hand it over to someone he could barely tolerate. Henry probably felt cut off from what, to him, was his entire life.

Nick had heard of men who retired after a lifetime of hard work, only to end up feeling useless and depressed, getting old before their time. Nick didn't want that for Henry, regardless of the animosity they usually shared.

What the hell. Maybe he would stay for dinner, after all.

When he arrived at Henry's twenty minutes later, the sight of Sammi's rust heap in the driveway gave him a wry smile. The lady obviously took her friendships seriously. It was plain to Nick that Sammi had come to make certain Henry wasn't alone tonight.

For a moment the urge to leave was strong. With Sammi here, Henry didn't need him for company. But no, Nick had come this far. It wouldn't hurt to go in for a few minutes. He hoped.

Maybe for once, with Sammi between them, he and Henry could be civil to each other. That last time, the day Sammi had been swimming, hadn't been too bad.

With a deep breath to brace himself for whatever lay ahead, Nick stepped out of his Lincoln and walked to the porch.

Henry answered the doorbell. "Nick! You said you couldn't make it. I didn't expect you."

117

Nick nodded toward Sammi's car. "I see you've already got company. I can come another time."

"No, no." Henry opened the storm door and motioned Nick inside. "Come on in. This is great."

The obvious enthusiasm in Henry's voice was such a far cry from the usual cynicism, at first Nick thought he'd only imagined it. But no, the look in Henry's eyes was definitely welcoming. It had been such a long, long time . . . Something in Nick's chest fluttered. Swallowing past the sudden lump in his throat hurt. "If you're sure," he managed.

"Of course I'm sure."

Nick stepped inside and followed Henry into the living room.

"Look who's here," Henry announced.

"Did you get the feeling they didn't want us around?" Sammi asked Nick as they took the sidewalk to the driveway an hour later.

Landscaping accent lights edged the flower bed next to the house and followed the sidewalk and the curve of the drive. One beamed up the trunk of the giant sycamore, the focal point of the front yard. But rather than intruding on the darkness, the lights complemented the night, a counterpoint to chirping crickets and singing cicadas.

With his mood better than it had been in a long time, Nick said, "They didn't exactly beg us to stick around for dessert."

He looked over at Sammi. She rolled her eyes, and the next thing he knew, they both broke out laughing.

"Oh, God," Sammi said. "I was never so embarrassed in my life as when Ernestine answered the door."

Nick found himself laughing again as Sammi told about holding daisies in front of her face and shouting "Surprise!"

It felt good to laugh.

"Did you know he had a girlfriend?" Sammi asked.

Nick shook his head. He had thought Sammi filled that role in Henry's life, until he'd learned better. "Believe me, you weren't any more surprised than I was. I had no idea he was seeing anyone."

"Me neither, but I'm glad he is."

Yeah. Nick was glad, too. He'd never seen his father with any woman but his mother, and that had been years ago. It felt surprisingly good to know Henry wasn't alone.

He stopped at the edge of the driveway and inhaled the sweet scent of honeysuckle from the yard next door. He would have leaned against Sammi's car, but feared the damn thing might collapse under his weight.

It felt especially pleasant to be in such a good

mood when leaving Henry's house. Good moods and Nick and Henry hadn't gone together in so many years it hurt to think about it.

"You and Henry seemed to get along well tonight."

"You're reading my mind. We got along fine, thanks to you and Ernestine," he said. "Then, too, I need to thank you for this afternoon in my office when you told me off. I guess maybe I needed it."

"Is that why you came tonight?"

He shrugged. "Yeah. I guess you made me feel guilty."

"Good."

At her emphatic nod, he laughed again.

"I know I'm sticking my nose into something that's none of my business, but —"

"It's never stopped you before."

She chuckled.

The sound, low and husky, did things to his breathing that it shouldn't, made him feel things he'd promised himself he wouldn't feel with this woman.

"No," she said, "I guess I do have trouble minding my own business. But I've always wondered why you and Henry are usually . . ."

"At each other's throat?"

"I would have said you were usually in disagreement."

His good mood was slipping. "That would

have been very diplomatic of you."

"Well, for father and son—"

"Cut it out, Sammi. Surely Henry has told you the truth."

"What truth? Henry hasn't told me anything."

"You mean he hasn't told you he's not my father? He hasn't told you what a good joke my mother thought it was to wait until I was seventeen years old before announcing I was some other man's bastard?"

Seven

Sammi was in bad trouble, and she knew it. Her ridiculous yearning—the one she still fought on a daily basis—to have Nick Elliott kiss her, to be held in his arms, was one thing. Now, ever since that night last week in Henry's driveway when Nick had told her Henry wasn't his father, now she found herself wanting to hold Nick in her arms, wanting to comfort him, to somehow ease the deep pain he tried constantly to hide. She couldn't imagine the hurt of learning the father who'd raised her all her life was in fact not her father after all.

The good side of the situation was that she and Nick seemed to be on better terms since that night. After donning safety glasses for a long overdue tour of the plant, Nick had even acknowledged how much he liked the new Video Jet paint marker.

"You mean we can keep it?" she had asked. Good Lord, she had actually batted her eyes at him! The mere memory made her groan. As far as she could remember, she'd never batted her eyes at a man in her life.

Nick had laughed. "I suppose we'll have to. If we tried to go back to the old way of marking, we'd have an employee revolt."

Sammi smiled at the memory. There had been several friendly exchanges like that in the past days. Maybe she and Nick really could be friends. Now that she understood him better, she was starting to genuinely like him.

She wondered if there was something she could do to bring Nick and Henry closer. Even if Henry wasn't Nick's biological father, the man had "raised him from a pup," as Sammi's grandfather would have said. Nick and Henry had apparently shared a close relationship before they learned the truth. It seemed to Sammi that their anger should have been directed at Mrs. Elliott all these years, rather than at each other.

Then again, maybe she should just stay out of it and let things sort themselves. The two men had actually been cordial with each other at Henry's last week. Maybe their long-standing animosity was finally dying out.

She was still thinking about Nick and Henry Thursday night, when she realized she needed to let Nick know about her trip to Chicago next week. Henry had known she was going, had told her she needed to go. But he probably hadn't mentioned it to Nick.

Sammi was both nervous and excited about attending her first International Machine and Tool Show at Chicago's famous McCormick Place Convention Center. This would also be her first stay in a luxury hotel; she'd heard the Palmer House was one of the best.

Viewing all the latest computerized machinery, complete with numerical controls and in some cases, laser beams, some of which could undoubtedly boost Elliott Air's production sky-high, all manufactured by the biggest and best machine and tool manufacturers from all over the world, well, the mere thought of it took her breath away. The Chicago IMT was held only every other year. She was so glad this was the year, that she wouldn't have to wait another twelve months to go. She wouldn't have been able to stand it!

But even that excitement paled beside one tiny little fact. Sammi Carmichael had never been outside the state of Oklahoma in her life. And while she had spent the past three years building parts for major aerospace giants such as Boeing, Lockheed, and McDonnell Douglas, who built the planes operated by major carriers, she had never even so much as stepped foot inside an airplane.

So many firsts! Her first flight, her first trip outside the state, her first trade show. No wonder she was nervous. And excited.

The next morning she got to work early. Not

having her own typewriter, she sat at Darla's desk and used the computer to draft a memo to Nick about her trip.

"Don't tell me you're after my job."

Sammi jumped a mile. She hadn't heard Darla come in. "You scared the daylights out of me. And no, I'm not after your job. Secretaries have to work too hard."

"Don't I know it." Darla grinned.

"I'm almost finished. I just have to print this off."

"I'll do it, if you want."

"Would you? Thanks, Darla, you're a gem. This is a memo to Nick about my trip next week. Henry knew about it, but I doubt Nick does. Just print it and lay it on his desk if he's not in."

"Sure, no problem." Darla looked at her watch. "Don't you need to meet with Production in a few minutes?"

"Yes, I'm due downstairs right now."

"Then scat."

Sammi grinned. "Yes, ma'am."

She thought about her upcoming trip several times during that day and the next, but more and more her thoughts turned back to Nick and Henry. As she left the building Friday evening, she decided this weekend would give her the opportunity to see if Nick and Henry's unofficial truce was holding. Since the company's annual Labor Day picnic was serving double duty this year, also being used as Henry's official retirement party, the two men would both be present. She would keep an eye on them. She hated the thought of the two of them fighting. Surely at the picnic they would be on their best behavior.

And it seemed she was right. Nick and Henry seemed relaxed at the picnic. The atmosphere was fun-filled and boisterous, the sun was bright, and the temperature was holding in the low nineties. The smell of barbecued brisket, roasting ears of corn, baked beans, and fresh bread drifted on the breeze beneath the blackjack trees and made Sammi's mouth water. From the drink table, the yeasty scent of beer fought with the tang of lemonade. The caterers did a brisk business as more than three hundred of the plant's employees gorged themselves.

Henry was in rare form, holding court over the fifty or so people surrounding his picnic table. Nick stood on the fringe of the crowd, eating from a paper plate. He laughed with the others at something Henry said, then walked off.

It was only the second time Sammi had seen Nick wearing something other than a suit, and once again, those tight denims affected her breathing. His white pullover set off his deep tan, and the wind kept tossing his hair down onto his forehead. She wanted desperately to smooth it back into place with her fingers.

Right then and there Sammi had a sharp lecture with herself. She and Nick had been getting along fine lately. She had no business having anything other than friendly thoughts about him. It would only lead to trouble and trouble she didn't need.

By the time she filled her plate, Nick was off in the grass roughhousing with a group of employees' children.

Ah, damn. He liked kids. She should have known.

Wasn't there anything about the man these days she didn't find appealing?

When she finished eating, she tossed her plate in the trash. It was time to do something she had put off much too long. She had to talk to Gus. She found him standing next to Darla watching a horseshoe pitching contest.

"Gus, can I talk to you for a minute?"

Gus looked at her and shrugged. "Guess so."

He followed her away from the crowd to relative privacy beneath a cottonwood.

"I want to apologize again for what happened last week," Sammi said. "I never really thanked you for fixing my car. And you never told me what I owe you."

With his hands stuffed into the hip pockets of his jeans, Gus beheaded a dandelion with the toe of his boot, studying the process intently rather than looking at Sammi. "Forget it."

"I won't. You know that. Come on, Gus, we've been friends a long time. I don't want you being angry with me. And I don't want you thinking Nick and I are . . . well, you know. There's nothing going on between us. You know me better than that."

"Ah, heck, Sammi, I know. I was just mouthing off. I'm sorry, too."

She held her hand out. "Friends?"

He accepted her offer of a handshake. "Friends."

They grinned at each other.

"Now what about my car? What do I owe you?"

He waved her question away. "You don't owe me anything. It was just a clogged fuel line. Didn't cost me anything to fix it. But damn, Sammi, when are you gonna get a new car? That thing's pitiful."

Sammi laughed. "Now you sound like Nick."

Gus started to respond, but Steve, the Director of Manufacturing, trotted toward them and yelled, "Come on, Sammi, we need a second baseman." When he reached them, he took her by the arm. "Come on."

She resisted his tug. "For what?"

"Production challenged the executive staff to a game. J. W. swears he won't play, so you have to. We need you plus both executive secretaries just to make a team."

"Marie and Darla agreed to this? After the way you guys razzed them last year?"

"Hey, Carmichael!" Nick called from the diamond. "Get out here!"

She turned back to Gus. "Guess I have to go play ball. You coming?"

"Softball in this heat? Not this old man."

"Old man, my foot."

Gus grinned. "I'll just heckle from the sidelines."

What ensued was a tough afternoon of rousing competition. Tough, because it was hard to hit or catch a ball when laughing. The game actually boiled down to which team told the best jokes. Someone produced a bullhorn, and every time a batter got ready to swing, an opposing team member would call out a joke.

Gus hollered out more than his fair share, trying to distract each executive staff member when he or she came up to bat.

The more personal the joke, the better the effect. When Sammi stepped up to bat in the second inning, Cal Harmon, who ran the new CNC Router on the second shift, called out, "Hey, Sammi! Know how to tell which computer terminal belongs to the redhead?"

Sammi hefted the bat and groaned. Cal was customizing a "blonde" joke specifically for her. She concentrated on her grip, determined not to start laughing.

"It's the one with whiteout on the screen!"

Sammi turned her head and made a face.

"Strike one!"

Production workers hooted and whistled.

"Pay attention out there, Carmichael!"

Nick. He was the only one who called her that.

After two strikes and a ball, Sammi finally managed to get on first. Bob Loflin, the company controller, hit her home.

Around about the fifth inning, the teams started running out of jokes and resorted to simply repeating the punch lines. By the sixth inning both sides were so exhausted from laughing they agreed to call the seven-seven game a tie.

Sammi felt a driving need to get away from Nick. All during the game he'd been chummy with her, like they were old pals. True, they'd been getting along better lately, but there had still been a slight distance between them. A necessary distance, if Sammi was to keep her wits about her.

What was it about her boss that kept her dreaming of impossible things? Things like kissing and—

Damn. She had to stop thinking of him in those terms before she drove herself crazy. She tossed her mitt into the box one of the production crew had brought and headed straight for the lemonade barrel.

Nick watched her walk away, faded jeans hugging her like a second skin. He could swear he felt his adrenaline rise just from the sight. A bead of sweat rolled down his temple and he brushed it aside.

Sammi in jeans, with her hair blowing wild

and free in the wind, dust and perspiration on her cheeks—God, what a sight. She tied him in knots without even trying. And she wasn't trying, he'd finally decided. She was just . . . just Sammi. No artifice, no pretense. Just open and friendly, when she let her guard down, that is.

He was just about to get her figured out. That ice maiden routine of hers made its appearance rarely these days, and then only when she was trying, for some reason, to hide her feelings. She hadn't pulled it on him since that day she'd called him names in his office.

Ah, what the hell. They were friends now. What could it hurt to spend a little extra time with her? He jogged to catch up with her. "You've got dirt all over your backside," he told her.

"I don't doubt it."

Look at her. He couldn't believe it. She was blushing. The last time he checked, it was still the late twentieth century. He couldn't remember when he'd seen a grown woman blush. Maybe never.

When she started dusting off the seat of her jeans, he couldn't resist teasing her a little. "Want any help with that?"

Her blush deepened.

"Sorry." He grinned. "It's just that those jeans . . . well, they, uh, they're not your usual office attire."

"What's wrong with my jeans?"

131

"Nothing! Nothing. In fact, they look . . . you look great in them."

"As opposed to how I look in my office attire?"

"I didn't say that. Don't put words in my mouth." She wasn't kidding. He couldn't believe it. She was bristling up right before his eyes like a threatened porcupine.

"What's wrong with the way I dress at work?"

She still wasn't kidding. She looked like she really wanted to know. Damn. How had he gotten himself into this mess? "Nothing's wrong with it." Sort of.

"But you don't like it."

He grinned again. "Let's just say I like you better in tight jeans."

The fleeting glimpse he got of her face before she turned away told him he'd blown it. She looked . . . hurt. And just when he'd thought he had her figured out.

"Hey, Sammi." He stepped up to her side.

She ducked her head. Nick bent down so he could see her face. "What's wrong? Hey, I was only teasing."

She sniffed, and in one smooth motion, raised her head and tossed her hair behind her shoulder.

There it was, that look he'd prided himself on not seeing for the past week—the ice maiden look. "What the hell? Sammi? What's going on? Why that look?"

"You were making fun of me, and I don't like it."

"Making . . . I was not!"

"Well what do you call it, then?"

Now it was Nick's turn to feel embarrassed. He only hoped like hell *he* wasn't blushing. Caught in the act like a gangly teenager, and now he had to confess. "I must be out of practice if you couldn't tell." He shrugged and gave her a wry grin. "I was flirting with you."

Her mouth and eyes popped open. She looked like she'd never heard of such a thing. He wanted to push her chin up with a forefinger, but refrained. There were too many eyes to see, too many tongues to wag. He settled for saying, "You'll catch flies."

"Stop it."

"Just trying to help."

She glared at him. What had he done now?

"I meant," she said with a clenched jaw, "stop making fun of me. I thought we were getting to be friends lately."

"I did, too, but I haven't got the slightest idea what's bugging you all of a sudden."

"What's bugging me is, I don't like being made a fool of. Flirting with me. Sure. We both know I'm not the type of woman men flirt with. I'm tired of being made fun of. Whatever game you're playing, go play with somebody else. I don't know the rules, and I'm not interested in learning."

Thunderstruck, all Nick could do was stand there in the glaring sun like an idiot and watch her stomp away. This time it was his mouth hanging open.

If he lived to be a thousand, he'd never understand women, most particularly, this woman, he thought, shaking his head at her retreating backside.

I'm not the type of woman men flirt with.
The hell she wasn't.

Nick remembered Sammi's words with frustration. What the devil had she meant by that? He'd tried to ask her, but by the time he'd gathered his wits and gone after her, her rusty excuse for a car was stirring up a wake of dust as it whipped out of the park's unpaved parking lot.

He wanted nothing more than to race after her and find out why a woman with her looks would think she wasn't worth flirting with, but he had obligations. He couldn't walk out on a park full of his own employees. He was, after all, the official host, if picnics had such things.

It was nine o'clock when he finally got home that night. He was hot and tired and smelled like the Dallas Cowboys' locker room right after halftime. And he was ticked off. With Sammi for taking his words and actions the wrong way, and for whatever she'd meant by her cryptic remark. With himself, too, for acting like a clumsy teenager and spoiling the easy mood he and Sammi had shared the past several days.

He should call her, find out what was going through that convoluted mind of hers. He got as far as looking up her number and writing it down on the pad beside his phone before changing his mind. Instead, he snatched a beer out of the refrigerator.

He had it half down when he picked up the phone again. After the first three digits he hung up.

Frustrated with himself for acting like an idiot, he peeled off his sweaty, dusty clothes and took a cool shower. Afterwards, with a towel hanging around his neck, he felt calmer. He picked up the phone and punched in Sammi's number. She answered on the third ring.

"If I hurt your feelings this afternoon, I'm sorry," he said.

"Who is this?"

"Very funny."

"Nick?"

"How many other men managed to hurt your feelings and make you mad today, without having any idea how they managed to do it?"

"It's late, Nick."

"It's nine-thirty. I want to know what you meant about men not flirting with you."

"Who's asking? My boss, or my former friend?"

"Now she's a comedian."

135

"Well?"

"What difference does it make?"

"Because if my boss is asking, it's none of his business. If it's my friend — former friend —"

"Just tell me what the hell you meant."

"I meant just what I said. I know men don't find me attractive, Nick."

"Men don't what?"

"If all your attention has been to make me feel good, it's sweet of you, but you don't have to bother. If you're making fun of me, it's not funny, and it has to stop. If you're just hard up for kicks, there are plenty of other women around who are more your type. Find one, please. Good night."

The next thing Nick heard was a dial tone buzzing in his ear.

Damn. She'd done it again. She'd left him speechless.

He didn't regain the ability to talk — in anything other than four-letter words, that is — until the next morning at work, when he found Sammi sitting at her desk.

She gave him a polite smile, the smile she might give a stranger. "Good morning."

"There's a friend of yours here who'd like to see you in my office right away."

She pushed her chair back and stood. "Who is it?"

Nick did his best to keep from grinding his teeth. For a friend, she jumped up off her chair.

For him, she turned on the ice. "It's a surprise."

From the look on her face, he knew she thought it might be Henry. She could just go on thinking that until he got her into his office. With the door shut.

They walked the long corridor side by side, his footsteps sounding hollow, her plain two-inch pumps ringing out sharply against the tile. As they passed Marie's desk, Nick told his secretary to hold his calls.

Sammi stepped into his office and stopped abruptly. "Where," she said, eyeing him suspiciously over her shoulder, "is this friend of mine?"

Nick closed the door, leaned back against it, and held his arms out from his sides. "Right here."

"Is this another one of your jokes?"

He dropped his arms. "No, it's not a joke. I'm not teasing, I'm not flirting, and I'm not making fun of you. I'm trying to be your friend, if you'll let me. But you're not leaving this office until you tell me how you can possibly think men don't find you attractive."

Sammi whirled and crossed to the window, her back to him, her arms hugging her chest.

Over her shoulder Nick saw Elliott Air's only remaining company-owned plane, the Skybird 2000 from the picture in the conference room, take off from the Wiley Post runway across the field. Jerry from Quality Control, on his way to see a client. He wouldn't be back until the end of the week.

Nick watched Sammi watch the plane, until it was out of sight. Then finally she said, "I can't believe you're doing this."

"And I can't believe you really think you're not attractive."

He moved until he stood a scant inch behind her.

He hadn't meant to do that. He'd meant this to be a down-to-earth, sane discussion. Standing this close to her, smelling the wildflower fragrance of her hair, he felt his sanity slipping away. "Maybe the men in your past were all blind. I'm not."

She turned and faced him, piercing him with her suspicious brown gaze. To her credit, she did not back away. "Are you trying to convince me you think I'm attractive?"

"Of course I think you are. Would I act the way I have around you if I didn't? If I weren't attracted to you, why would I have kissed you?"

She swallowed hard and stared somewhere in the region of his throat. "I . . . My clothes aren't nice. My hair . . ." She smoothed a loose strand back. Her fingers shook.

Nick gently pushed her hand away. "Camouflage."

"What?" She looked at him then, her brow wrinkled in confusion.

"These suits that don't fit, your hair pulled

138

back so tight, they're camouflage, that's all, and not very good camouflage, at that." He reached behind her head and searched for pins, pulling them out one by one, running his fingers through her wild, glorious hair until it fanned out across her shoulders.

"What are you doing?" Her voice was thin and weak.

He leaned toward her. "Something I probably shouldn't, something I promised I wouldn't."

"Why?" She licked her lips, and he nearly groaned aloud.

He couldn't take his gaze from her moist lips and that tiny, sexy mole at the corner of her mouth. "Because you're the flame—" He held her face in both hands, his fingers threading into the soft thickness of her hair, and traced her satin smooth cheeks with his thumbs. He brushed her lips with his. "And I'm the moth."

Eight

His lips brushed hers again, slower this time, softer, but more deliberate. Sammi felt her knees go weak. Oh God, what was he doing to her? What was she letting him do?

His tongue teased her lips.

She gasped.

His hands tightened on her cheeks and his mouth took hers firmly, fiercely, stirring a hunger deep inside her. A wild, terrifying yearning almost burning through her, from head to toe.

Could it be true? Could Nick really find her good-looking?

So what if he does? You're surely not the only woman he's attracted to.

The intruding thought brought pictures to mind of Nick in the arms of someone else. A stabbing pain shot through her heart. "No!" She wrenched away from him.

He released her so fast she nearly fell. "No," she whispered again, her breath coming in hard gasps.

He brushed a strand of hair from her cheek. She flinched at his electrifying touch.

He dropped his hand and studied her a long minute. "No?" he asked, reaching for her again.

"No." Panicked, Sammi backed away. She couldn't let him touch her again. If he did . . . "No." She shook her head.

Nick raised his hands in a gesture of surrender and backed away. "All right. No, it is. I've shown you how I feel. The next move is yours. From now on it's strictly business between us until you tell me otherwise."

Sammi rubbed a sudden chill from her arms. "I think we've had this conversation before."

"Similar, yes. But before, I think I was as confused as you were."

"You're not confused now?"

He shook his head slowly, his hot blue gaze scorching her face. "No, I'm not. Now I know exactly what I want."

Sammi was finally regaining control of her breathing, if not her shaking. She tossed her hair behind her shoulders. "What is that, Nick? Some sleazy little office affair squeezed in between lunch and your next staff meeting?"

As he stepped toward her, his jaw hardened. "You're confusing me with other men again. Is that what he did? Your husband?"

Sammi stood her ground. She had to. "This isn't about anyone else, it's about you and me.

You, the man of the world, and me, the farm girl from Stillwater, Oklahoma. Not anyone else. Just us."

"There is no us. You just said so. But in answer to your question, I know exactly what I want, and it's not some sleazy little office affair, as you put it."

"Then what do you want?" *Dumb question, Sammi.*

"You." He traced a finger along her lower lip. "And I think," he added softly, "you want me, too."

Her heart pounded beneath her breastbone. Sammi didn't know how to answer such a bald statement. Her first thought was of denial, but it would be false. She did want him. Desperately. But she knew from experience that the heat of passion soon blew out. He would get tired of her. After all, what did she have to offer him but inadequacies as a female, as a woman. She hoped to never face that again.

And when he got tired of her, as he soon would, Sammi would be the one out on the street looking for a new job, her heart in pieces.

Her job was her life and her salary was her salvation. She could not afford to risk either. Not for anything. No matter how tempting the man before her might be. Nick was right about that. She did want him. And maybe he really wanted her, for now. But whatever he was offering wasn't worth the risk. She took a deep breath.

"Actually—" She pulled her hair back to her nape. "—all I really want from you is the use of a comb."

His eyes widened, then quickly narrowed to angry slits. "I guess my first impression of you was right. You are one cold-blooded lady."

Sammi raised her chin a notch, determined not to let it quiver.

"A man spills his guts, and all you can think about is how your hair looks. The ice maiden liveth. Here." With sharp movements, he pulled a short black comb from the inside pocket of his jacket and slapped it against her palm. "Keep it, with my blessing."

As he whirled around and stormed to his desk, Sammi's vision blurred. *Oh, God, don't let me cry. Not here, not now, please.*

With shaking fingers, she did her best to comb her hair. She located only two of the four pins Nick had removed, but they would have to do. She could not walk out of this office with her hair down. She never wore her hair down at work.

Her hair finally in some semblance of order, she dared a glance across the room. Nick sat at his desk reading what looked like a manufacturing report.

And he called her cold-blooded. Here she

stood, trembling, while he calmly went back to work as though nothing momentous had happened.

The next move was hers, was it? All right. She walked out of his office and back to her own, where she belonged. On her way out the door she tried for grace and dignity but settled for speed.

Marie raised an eyebrow, perhaps in question of Sammi's haste, or her flushed face. Sammi ignored her. She reached her office and once inside, closed the door with great care. Then she sank onto her chair and buried her face in her hands.

Why now? she wondered. Why with this man did she find something so rare and beautiful? Why him?

Just moments ago in his office, before she'd come to her senses, she had felt herself wanting to please him, make him happy. She knew where that led. Next she'd be letting him control her every action, just the way she had let Jim. Then, like Jim, Nick would grow tired of her and look for a more exciting woman.

She couldn't go through that again.

The last time, with Jim, it had meant losing her home and having to get a job. This time she would lose her job. She wouldn't be able to work with Nick day after day, still wanting him when he no longer wanted her.

But there was nowhere for her to go and receive anywhere near the salary she now made, and she couldn't afford to give up her new salary. With her next paycheck she would be able to pay off three of the four remaining debts Jim had left her.

Then, when that last one was paid off in a few months—freedom! Of course, she could have a measure of freedom now, if she were willing to forego putting money from every paycheck into her savings account. But the thought of being without any financial backup again terrified her.

No, she would rather do without and know she had money for an emergency than to spend her hard-earned money on things she didn't really need.

Of course, she really did need a new car. And maybe some nicer clothes? No, clothes could wait. But her trusty old Ford wasn't going to last much longer; she would have to replace it.

Which meant she had to keep her job.

Which meant she had to stay away from Nick Elliott. The man could easily have her eating out of his palm in no time at all if she succumbed to his wishes. Then he would never take her seriously again. She wouldn't be a valued member of his executive staff, she would be his lover.

Lover.

The word sent streamers of want and hunger shimmering through her.

"Oh, Nick," she whispered. "Why you? Why now?"

Why couldn't she have fallen for someone other than her boss?

Fallen for? Is that what she'd done? Was she in love with Nick Elliott? *Please, God, no.*

She wouldn't love him, she wouldn't want him. That's all there was to it. He said they would keep things strictly business. Fine. That's the way it should be. She could do that. She could. She hoped.

During the next several days Nick was as good as his promise. Not by word, deed, or look did he cross the "strictly business" line. Sammi was both relieved and disappointed. The latter emotion made her angry with herself. After all, she was the one who'd told him no to a personal relationship.

Not that she thought he'd been all that serious anyway. If he had been, wouldn't he be having a little more trouble than she'd seen staying away from her? If he really wanted her, would he have given up so easily?

She had the sinking sensation that she had been right all along. Nick had only been playing a game with her. The idea hurt, but then so did a lot of things in life. She would get over it.

Thursday was set for the out-of-state company to conduct the in-house demonstration of their new Theodolite System. As he had promised, Nick attended the demo. Sammi kept her fingers crossed, and everything went without a hitch. The system appeared to be all Sammi had been led to believe.

Friday, Nick was ready for her report and projections in anticipation of purchasing the system. When she showed up at his office with her paperwork, he looked at his watch.

"I don't mean to put you off," he said, "but I'm starved. Can we do this over lunch, or would you rather wait until this afternoon?"

A smart woman would have told him the afternoon would have been fine. But Sammi was so determined to convince him, and herself, that Nick no longer had any effect on her, she found herself agreeing to his suggestion.

He gave her a crooked grin. "Thanks."

Sammi frowned. "For what?"

"For trusting me enough to go to lunch with me."

She looked away, not able to decide whose behavior she needed to worry about, his, or hers.

"Come on," Nick cajoled. "My treat. I'm starved. I feel like a steak."

To lighten the mood, Sammi said, "You don't look like a steak."

Then he did it. He flashed those damn, wicked dimples at her. Her heart started pounding. "Uh, let me get my briefcase so I don't have to carry all these loose files," she said. "I'll meet you out front."

Nick drove her in his smooth-riding Lincoln down Northwest Expressway to Steak and Ale. Sammi wondered how many business meetings had been held, how many deals cut beneath the beamed ceilings of the restaurant. How many racehorses bought and sold—or, in Oklahoma's boom days, how many oil wells—in front of the salad bar or over a juicy steak.

She needn't have worried about her lunch with Nick turning into a disaster. Her own enthusiasm for the Theodolite System kept their lunch discussion lively and on track. She was pleased to realize Nick was almost as excited about the system as she was.

"How long will it take us to get a return on our investment?"

Sammi tapped the lower half of the paper beside his plate. "I've estimated the ROI to be paid up in three years."

"Is that as conservative an estimate as the three-year ROI you turned in on the CNC Router?"

Sammi grinned while slicing off another chunk of the restaurant's distinctive brown bread. "It better be."

"And if it's not?"

"Then I'll still be on target with the three-year estimate, but I'll lose my bet with myself." She slathered her bread with honey butter, then took a bite. Ah . . . ambrosia.

Nick sat back and let the waitress refill his coffee. "You bet with yourself?" he asked Sammi. "What do you get if you win?"

"Nothing extravagant, I assure you."

"Knowing you, extravagant is probably something really wild, like a new toothbrush."

She gave him a mock glare. "I think I'm insulted."

"I think if you don't turn loose of some of that money you're making and buy yourself a new car, you're going to end up walking to work."

"You've got me there."

"You're kidding. You're getting a new car?"

"Eventually."

"Before winter, please?"

Sammi laughed. "Afraid I'll be begging rides from you?"

"I'm afraid," he said with a frown, "you're going to end up stranded somewhere in the middle of the night when no one's around. And for heaven's sake, when you do get a car, get one that's not used."

She made a face. "Are you having a good time spending my money?"

149

"Hell, I might as well. You don't seem to be spending any of it. What do you do, stuff it under your mattress?"

"Quit picking on me."

"All right." He raised his hands in surrender. "But you still haven't told me what your bet with yourself was for."

She gave him a dramatic sigh. She wasn't about to tell him her bet was for new underwear. "You were right. It was a new toothbrush."

Nick nearly choked on his coffee.

But Sammi was already thinking of other things. This lunch had gone well. She hadn't been a bit uncomfortable around Nick, and he seemed equally at ease in her company. They had talked business, then nonsense, but nothing really personal.

Would what she was thinking really work? Would Nick consider attending the National Business Aircraft Association meeting at the end of October? Could she and Nick make an out-of-town trip together and keep the atmosphere impersonally friendly? If they could, the New Orleans meeting might just be the perfect way to convince him it was time for Elliott Air to re-enter the aircraft manufacturing business and build their own planes again.

"Yoohoo, Sammi." Nick waved a hand in front of her face. "Is anybody in there?"

"What? Oh, yeah. Sorry, my mind was wandering." She tucked her napkin beside her plate and started stuffing files back into her briefcase. "When will you decide on the Theodolite System?"

"When we get back to the office, leave your documentation with me. I'll talk it over with Henry."

Surprised, Sammi raised a brow.

"We do talk, sometimes," he said with a grin. "And he is still the owner of the company."

"Let me rephrase my question then," Sammi said. "Do you like the system? Do you think we should get it?"

"Yes. Yes, to both questions. You should congratulate yourself. You've done a good job with this project."

"Does that mean you'd be willing to call off my ninety-day probation?"

He grinned. "Not if it keeps you working this hard."

"That's not funny, Elliott."

"Don't worry about the probation, Carmichael. You're not going to end up on the street over it."

"Easy for you to say."

"I'm serious. The nature of your probation has changed."

Sammi clasped her hands in her lap to keep from fidgeting. "Changed how?"

"It's obvious to me that you and your job are assets to the company."

Sammi's heart gave a little leap of joy.

"What remains to be seen," Nick said, "is if Advanced Technology should remain a separate department, or if it should be placed under Manufacturing Engineering."

"Placed under J. W.? You can't mean that!"

Nick narrowed his eyes. "Why can't I?"

"By taking away my status of director, my equal rank with the other staff members, you strip me of all authority," she cried.

"And putting me under J. W.—you know I like him, but you also know what he thinks of my projects. Once the new equipment is purchased and up and running, he thinks it's great. But up until then, he thinks every idea I have is frivolous and unnecessary. If I have to get his approval on everything I do, you might as well fire me and abolish my job, because none of my ideas will ever get past J. W."

"Don't you think you're being unfair?"

"No, I don't. And I can't see what difference it should make to you whether I'm a director or not. Unless you're looking for a reason to cut my salary."

"This has nothing to do with your salary."

"Then why are you talking about demoting me?"

"I'm not out to demote you or strip you of

152

your salary and title. I'm trying to streamline the operations department. Since Frank retired as Vice President of Operations, and Henry didn't see fit to replace him, I'm having to handle Frank's job as well as mine. I think the fewer people who have to report directly to me, the smoother things will run."

Sammi felt her heart sink. "And I'm the only director without a staff, so I'm the most easily done away with."

Nick pursed his lips. "Done away with is not a phrase I would have used." He shook his head. "Look, Sammi, none of this is cast in stone. I haven't made a decision yet, so don't worry about it. I might just as easily decide to hire a new Vice President of Operations."

Sammi rubbed at the sudden ache in her forehead. "How likely are you to promote one of the current directors?"

"That would be my first preference."

Sammi gave the idea some thought. "With his background and experience, J. W. is the most likely candidate. Just for the record," she said, "I wouldn't mind working for him if he were vice president."

"Why not?" Nick asked with a frown. "You would still have to report to him rather than me."

"Yes, but I would still be a director, equal to the other directors. J. W. takes my title a lot more seriously than he takes me. And as a director, I wouldn't have to ask his permission for everything I did."

"You would still be working for him."

"But I wouldn't be just another employee. I'd be head of my own department. A director. He would respect that and take me more seriously."

Nick gave her a half-grin. "So it's all right with you if I promote him?"

Sammi grimaced. "Is that what I sounded like? Like I was giving you permission?"

Nick laughed. "No. Don't worry about it."

"I'm sorry," Sammi said. "It's just that my job is important to me, Nick."

"So I gathered. But as I said, don't worry about it."

"And as I said," she told him. "That's easy for you to say."

Sammi spent the rest of the day trying not to think about what her job would be like if she lost her title and had to answer to J. W.

To be fair, though, she feared if she lost her title she would have the same problems she had described to Nick no matter which director she ended up working for.

The entire idea was too depressing to dwell on.

That evening—her last at work before leaving

for Chicago—Sammi stayed late to write Nick a memo about the NBAA Convention in New Orleans. He could think about the convention while she was out of town, but he wouldn't be able to give her a flat-out no. When she got back, she would have an entire month to convince him to go.

She stuffed the memo into an envelope and, instead of leaving it on Marie's desk or in the mail room, she slid it under Nick's locked door.

On her way home she stopped at Henry's for a visit. He gave her stern advice regarding her trip.

"On the plane, keep your seat belt fastened even when the light goes out. In Chicago, take time away from the exhibits to do a little shopping. And I don't mean window shopping. Open that tight fist of yours and spend some money, girl. Buy something for yourself. Something frivolous."

"Have you been talking to Nick?"

"What does Nick have to do with this?"

"Never mind."

"Are you going to do as I say, young lady?"

She gave him a sharp salute. "Yessir."

Sammi went home, but was too excited to get much sleep. She wondered what Nick would say if she called him just to talk.

Bad idea.

Right. She was over him, anyway. They were friends again.

Saturday, Sammi packed, unpacked, and repacked at least a half-dozen times. Sunday morning she parked her car at Whinery's long-term parking and took the shuttle to the airport. She checked her luggage at the ticket counter, and at eight-fifteen showed her boarding pass to the flight attendant. With heart knocking and palms sweating, she stepped aboard her very first plane.

All the way down the isle to her seat she kept telling herself that the Boeing 757 was one of the safest aircraft in the world. After all, hadn't she, herself, made some of the parts for these very planes?

And you expect it to fly?

"Come on, Sammi," she said under her breath. "Planes do that all day every day. Accidents are a lot less frequent in the air than they are on the ground."

She was almost sorry J. W. and Steve weren't going with her. But as the other two members of the executive staff who normally attended trade shows, J. W. and Steve had elected to go to the International Machine and Tool Show Los Angeles convention earlier in the year.

On second thought, she was glad they weren't with her. She didn't want anyone at Elliott Air to see her nervousness.

She did wish, sadly, that Nick was beside her, that he really was attracted to her, that he cared

156

for her. That they were spending the next few days in Chicago together.

She smiled and shook her head. If Nick were with her, she would be so worried about what he really thought of her, she wouldn't have time to be jittery about flying.

But by the time she was buckled into her seat, the roar of the revving engines lost its sinister pitch and took on the timbre of excitement. She, Samantha Carmichael, was going to fly!

And she did. By the time the plane touched down at O'Hare two hours later Sammi decided she was born to fly. She was disappointed the flight had been so short. On the way home Friday, she was being routed home to Will Rogers World Airport by way of Dallas-Fort Worth. That meant she would be in the air longer. She could hardly wait.

At O'Hare Sammi took the escalator down to the baggage claim area. The wait for her luggage seemed eternal, but finally it came. She breathed a sigh of relief that her bag hadn't been sent on a trip of its own to some other city.

She had only brought one suitcase, so she hefted it off the conveyor belt and made her way through throngs of people still waiting for their luggage.

Outside she saw she had several choices of transportation: any one of a dozen different buses and shuttles, or a cab. She had never ridden in a cab. Having always had her own car, she'd never had the need.

"Taxi, ma'am?"

Sammi grinned. "Yes."

The driver, a tall, muscular man with a musical Jamaican accent, stowed her suitcase in the trunk, then held the back door open for her.

A moment later the cab pulled away from the curb and entered a stream of traffic that awed Sammi with its sheer density. The drive to the hotel might prove scarier than the plane ride.

The country mouse goes to town.

Sammi paused at the thought. That was the first time in days Jim's voice had taunted her. Maybe he was finally ready to leave her alone.

Or maybe she was finally letting go of her anger with him.

Now there was a sobering thought. Was that what that taunting voice in her head was all about? Was it her subconscious way of letting the past get to her so she could blame Jim for her troubles? So she could stay angry with him?

"Too deep, Sammi."

"You say something, miss?" the cab driver asked.

Sammi leaned toward the front seat to yell over the squawk of his two-way. "Just admiring the city."

He gave her a brief, cock-eyed look in the rearview mirror. "Yes, ma'am."

Sammi leaned back against the seat. She was in Chicago, Illinois, on business. And suddenly feeling full of herself, she thought with a grin.

The driver turned the volume down on his two-way and asked where Sammi was from. When she told him, he asked if Oklahoma City was as large as Chicago.

"In square miles, probably," she said. "But not in people. We don't have nearly the number of people. And—oh, look! A train, right out in the median! We don't have passenger trains."

For the rest of the ride, Sammi was amazed by the driver's open friendliness and the obvious pride he took in showing his city to a visitor. When they finally reached the downtown area— at home it would have taken ten minutes—here it took more than thirty—he pointed out the Daley Center, the Hancock Observatory, and other buildings. The top of the Sears Tower was lost in a low-hanging cloud.

"Have you ever seen Lake Michigan?" he asked.

"I've never seen anything outside of Oklahoma."

The driver looked at her with a mixture of horror and pity, as though she'd just admitted to never having tasted ice cream. He turned off the meter and headed north along Michigan Avenue. There Sammi got a closer view of the John Hancock Center, the Water Tower, and the 900 North

Michigan Shops before the driver turned east and took her to Lakeshore Drive.

When he turned south, Sammi gasped. On her right were more buildings, a park, Northwestern University. But on her left — Lake Michigan! So much water, she couldn't see the opposite shore. The overcast sky met the gray of Lake Michigan somewhere, she was sure, but the two blended together until, in the distance, she couldn't tell where one stopped and the other started. Fascinated, she stared in awe.

Yes, she thought, she was feeling quite full of herself, as if she alone were somehow responsible for Chicago's existence, the huge buildings, the never-ending lake. They had all been placed just so for her enjoyment. And enjoy them she would. She might even be so bold as to take Henry's advice and spend some money. Something about Chicago made her feel . . . daring.

Surely after three years of struggling and toeing the mark, she had earned the right to be a little frivolous with her money.

Her last thought as the cab pulled up before the Palmer House at State and Monroe was of Nick. He would be proud of her frivolous thoughts.

She didn't even flinch when the driver told her her fare came to twenty-five dollars.

* * *

Nick found Sammi's memo when he unlocked his office Monday morning. She wanted him to attend the NBAA meeting in New Orleans; would he please think about it?

He shook his head and chuckled. It had to be a coincidence. She couldn't be so attuned to him that she knew how badly he wanted an excuse to go to the meeting. But an excuse was all it would be, because even when Elliott Air had built planes, as Sammi wanted them to do again, they had built personal planes, not business jets. The NBAA was out of their league.

The last line of her memo brought him up short.

I'd like to discuss the possibility with you when I return from Chicago next week.

Chicago?

Then he realized why she was there. He felt stupid for not remembering the IMT. Of course she would go there.

But Chicago? Sammi? The farm girl from Stillwater, Oklahoma?

Then he relaxed. J. W. and Steve would take care of her, show her the ropes. Still, Nick knew he would worry about her until she got back. Why hadn't she mentioned the trip earlier?

Before he got sidetracked at his desk, he went down the hall to Operations. "Darla, would you make yourself a note to have Sammi see me as soon as she gets back from Chicago?"

"Sure, Nick."

"Speaking of Sammi, does she remember she's supposed to check out that new deburring machine while she's up there?"

Nick turned slowly toward the gravelly voice.

"Sammi doesn't tell me what she remembers, J. W. None of you do," Darla said.

"What are you doing here?" Nick demanded.

J. W. looked affronted. "Where else would I be?"

Easy, Elliott, easy. "Sorry. I just thought you'd be in Chicago with Sammi."

"Nah. Steve and I went to the L.A. show. Besides," he added with a touch of sarcasm, "with all the new equipment we've been buying lately, there can't be that much left to see."

Nick raised a brow. "Meaning?"

J. W. paused a moment, then shrugged. "Meaning nothing. Everything Sammi has recommended has worked out great. Besides, she's a big girl. She doesn't need Steve or me tagging along in Chicago. We'd probably just be in her way."

Nick wasn't convinced, but he let the subject drop. The trade show had started that morning and would be over Thursday. Sammi would be home by Friday. Just a week. He tried not to worry about her.

Later that evening when he stopped by Henry's to discuss the Theodolite System, Nick still

162

wasn't comfortable with Sammi being in Chicago alone. He suspected his concern had more to do with missing her than really worrying about her—after all, women traveled all over the world without some man to take care of them—but the idea of missing her was so hard to admit, he ignored it.

"What are you doing here?" Henry demanded.

Well, so much for the lull in hostilities. Henry was back in rare form, and Nick wasn't even in the door yet. "I told you I'd be over soon to discuss a new piece of equipment."

"You told me." Henry stepped aside to let Nick enter. "But when you didn't come over the weekend, I figured I wouldn't see you until next week. Why aren't you in Chicago?"

Ignoring that Chicago was precisely where he wanted to be, Nick said, "Isn't that what we're paying Sammi for?"

"You mean you sent her up there into that den of confusion and hype all by herself?"

"I didn't send her anywhere. I didn't even realize she was going until she was gone."

"Well, who went with her? I never would have let her go alone."

Another slur on Nick's management style. "Sammi's a big girl, Henry. With all she's accomplished at the plant in the past three years, surely this can't be her first trade show."

"Surely it is," Henry said. "It's also her first

trip outside the state of Oklahoma, probably her first trip anywhere by herself. And I know for a fact she has never been on a plane before."

"You're kidding. The woman who's so adamant about us building our own aircraft has never even flown?"

"Building? Who's building planes?"

"We are, if Sammi has her way."

Henry grinned. "No kidding. I knew that girl had a head on her shoulders. So what are you going to do about it?"

"I'm going after her, that's what I'm going to."

"What's that got to do with manufacturing planes?"

"Not a damn thing." Nick tossed Henry the file he had brought on the Theodolite System. "Here's her latest project. Look it over. I'll get back to you Friday or Saturday."

"Friday or Saturday?"

"When I'm home from Chicago. Who's our pilot these days?"

"Mark Heywood. You taking the Skybird?"

"I thought I would. Don't you think it's time our Director of Advanced Technologies took a ride in an Elliott aircraft?"

On his way down the driveway a few minutes later, Nick wished he knew precisely what that odd grin of Henry's had meant. Not that it really mattered. Nick was going after Sammi no matter what anyone thought. Good God. The farm girl from Stillwater, on the loose, and alone, in Chicago, when she'd never been away from home before.

Compared to Chicago, Oklahoma City, with one-third the population, was a small town. Visions of big city muggers and rapists and con men had him gripping the steering wheel all the way home.

He knew he wouldn't sleep that night for worrying about her.

Nine

Tuesday morning Nick's eyes felt like they each held a pound and a half of grit. He hadn't slept at all. He reached Heywood by phone, and the pilot readily agreed to fly Nick to Chicago that afternoon.

Asking Heywood to fly him hadn't been easy for Nick. For one pilot to ask another to fly him somewhere went against the grain. But Nick acknowledged he hadn't flown in months. That, combined with no sleep and a mind he couldn't seem to keep on track, spelled disaster in the air.

He would use the time during the flight to review the latest production figures. That is, if he could keep his mind off Sammi long enough.

Maybe going after her was a bad idea. With the way she continued to occupy his thoughts day and night, did he really trust himself to be with her away from work, away from everything familiar to them both?

166

Yet, after Sammi's reaction to his last pathetic fumble, Nick shouldn't have a thing to worry about. If he got out of line, she would set him straight in a minute. In fact, if he made any more moves on her, she was likely to take his head off. She seemed perfectly content with a friendly relationship. He would have to accept that.

Maybe he wouldn't stay, he thought. Maybe he would just check up on Sammi, make sure she was all right, then go home.

Then maybe, you jackass, you should have just called her.

When Heywood landed the Skybird at Chicago Midway, Nick was disgusted to realize he'd spent the entire flight thinking about Sammi. He had nursed one scotch and water all the way there, and hadn't accomplished a lick of work.

"With the trade show in town, the Palmer House isn't going to have a vacancy," Mark warned.

"Yes they will." Nick hadn't chased Sammi all this way to be sent across town to find a room.

At the Palmer House, the paunchy, middle-aged desk clerk shook his head. "I'm sorry, sir. We're booked solid."

Nick flashed his gold credit card in one hand and a fifty-dollar bill in the other. "Are you sure?"

"Well . . . let me look again." After a lengthy search via computer, the clerk said, "It looks like we've had a cancellation, but it's for a suite."

I'll bet, Nick thought. There were probably one or two cancellations for regular rooms, too, regular rooms with regular rates. But the man knew he had Nick over a barrel.

"We'll take it."

Mark carried their bags on up to the suite. Nick turned back to the clerk and asked if Sammi was registered.

The man flashed his teeth and ran a hand over his balding head. Without so much as a glance at the computer screen, he said, "Yes, sir, she sure is."

And Sammi thought men weren't attracted to her. The old goat behind the counter was practically drooling at the mention of her name.

"Is she in?" Nick asked.

"She went downstairs to shop about a half hour ago. Hasn't come back up yet."

Nick clenched his jaw. "You keep this close a tab on all your guests?"

The man's grin didn't slip a notch. "No sir. Only the special ones."

Nick left before he was tempted to say something he might regret.

"Only the special ones," he muttered. If the man paid more attention to his job than his female guests—

Nick ground his teeth and took the escalator to the Lower Arcade, his mood in direct contrast to the quiet dignity of the Palmer House lobby behind him. The deep green carpeting, dark, massive wood paneling and polished brass fixtures spoke of tradition and timeless quality. Of elegance and refinement.

Nick's mood was anything but elegant or refined. When he stepped off the escalator, he ground his teeth harder. The arcade was lined with shops. He would never find Sammi.

With a shrug, he started walking. Might as well take a look while he was there. He glanced in one store window after another, searching for the tall auburn-haired woman he couldn't seem to get off his mind.

And then he saw her. She stood before a mirror in an exclusive dress shop. Sammi. But it was a Sammi Nick had never seen before, except in his dreams.

His breath hung in his chest, while a deep, sudden need, both physical and emotional, nearly strangled him.

She pivoted on a spiked heel high enough to bring her almost to his eye level. The three-sided mirror before her shot back dazzling images of a lovely woman whose fiery cloud of auburn hair hung in loose waves over bare creamy shoulders. Every wild strand looked like it had just been run through the fingers of a man caught in the grip of passion.

The dress she wore was enough—or so little!—to stop his heart. From where he stood, the turquoise fabric looked like silk and clung to every supple curve of her luscious body, from just above her breasts to where it ended at least a hand's width—a large hand—above her knees. His heart kicked in and tried to pound its way right out of his chest.

The tight fabric stretching over her hips and around that shapely backside emphasized the bareness of what seemed like a mile and a half of legs. The long tight sleeves emphasized the bareness of her shoulders. The plunging neckline had him holding his breath for fear she would spill out of it.

Nick struggled to keep from moaning aloud. He had to hand it to her. When the lady finally decided to drop the camouflage of ill-fitting clothes and an unattractive hairstyle, she went, as they said at home, whole-hog. He had always thought her attractive, had known she was beautiful. But as she stood before the mirror in that dress, she was the most striking woman he'd ever seen in his life.

And he wanted her. Hotly, fiercely craved her. He wanted to wrap his arms around her and lose himself in her heat. He wanted to hold her all night long and wake holding her the next morning. And the next. And the next.

He shouldn't have come to Chicago. Having come anyway, he should turn around right this minute and go home. Instead, when Sammi disappeared into the back of the store, he walked toward the entrance and leaned against the wall across the hall from the shop. A moth waiting for his own personal flame.

Sammi opened the door to the dressing room and stepped inside.

"If you don't buy that dress and make some lucky man's entire year, it will be a crime," the salesclerk said. "May I show you anything else?"

Sammi looked around at the clothing draped over the chair, the bench and hanging from all four wall hooks. "No, thanks. I'm going to have enough trouble making up my mind as it is."

"Just call if you need anything." The salesclerk backed out of the tiny cubicle and closed the door behind her.

Sammi leaned a shoulder against the wall and sighed. A huge smile flashed back at her from three mirrored walls. She had never had so much fun in her life as she'd had trying on clothes for the past hour. The styles and colors, suggested by the salesclerk, were ones she had never tried before. They made her feel freer somehow, more exciting, more sure of herself. They made her feel good and, even in her humble opinion, look good.

She shook her head. "Henry, this is all your fault." She knew she was going to end up buying something, but she now had to choose from among the eight outfits she had tried on.

She shouldn't feel guilty about spending the money. She had diligently spent the past three years carefully paying on Jim's debts. Now with her new salary, she could still pay off Jim's debts and, by skipping this month's deposit to her savings account, buy a little something for herself.

A little something?

Well, okay, so the clothes were expensive. So she had already purchased all new makeup and had paid an exorbitant price to have the ends of her hair trimmed. So she'd paid another equally sky-high price for her very first manicure. Being away from home made her feel . . . defiant. She felt like breaking loose and doing something crazy. Besides, she'd done all that yesterday afternoon when she first arrived.

Still, if this wasn't crazy, she didn't know what was. She had walked the exhibit hall all day. By the time she left at five, her feet had been killing her. They still were. Yet she didn't care. She was having too much fun to let a little thing like screaming feet slow her down. She took a deep breath and picked up the closest outfit.

After another half hour of dithering, she decided on the turquoise dress and matching shoes. Lord, when would she ever have the occasion—or the nerve—to wear such a dress? And she would take a coordinated legging and long sweater set. The matching heels actually made her feet look almost dainty despite their swollen condition. She decided to wear the leggings, sweater, and matching shoes out of the store.

When the salesclerk ran the little red light beam over Sammi's credit card, Sammi forced herself to breathe deeply. Jim would have made her feel guilty, but he was gone. She could spend her own money on herself if she wanted. It wasn't as if she didn't have it.

She had another bad moment as she signed the charge slip and caught a glimpse of the total amount.

Then it was done. Wearing her new outfit, she picked up the bag containing the dress and headed for the door.

"Please come again," the salesclerk said.

No doubt the woman worked on commission and she knew a sucker when she saw one. Sammi merely smiled, thanked her for her help, and stepped out of the shop. She turned to head for the escalator when a deep, familiar voice halted her.

"Damn, lady, when you drop your camouflage, you really drop it, don't you?"

She whirled around toward the voice, giddy and scared at the same time. "Nick! What are you doing here?"

His gaze skimmed her up and down. "I came for the show."

The fire that leapt to life in his eyes as he

leaned casually against the wall burned away all her doubts about the money she had spent. Under the heat of his blue eyes she suddenly felt, for the first time in years, like a beautiful woman. A desirable woman.

"You look . . . great."

Something wild and new broke loose inside her. Yesterday she might have blushed and stammered. She certainly would have doubted either his vision or his honesty. This evening she smiled and said, "Thank you." Because right then, she felt great.

Nick pulled away from the wall and walked toward her. With a nod to the sack in her hands he asked, "What else did you buy?"

She pulled a turquoise sleeve out the top of the bag and waved it at him. "A new dress."

Something she didn't understand flickered in Nick's eyes. "Before you remind me we're only friends and business associates," he said, "I have one more personal remark I feel obliged to make."

Cautious yet curious, Sammi waited.

Frowning, Nick said, "If that's the dress you tried on about a half hour ago, don't ever wear it around me."

Crushed, her feelings hurt, Sammi asked, "Why would you say something like that? You've never even seen the dress."

"I saw you wearing it when you came out to look in those mirrors."

174

"You didn't like it?" It had been her favorite!

"Like it? No, I don't think like was what I felt at all. Let's just put it this way. If you ever wear that dress around me, I'll take it as an open invitation."

She felt her chin jutting out. "To what?"

The fire in his eyes burned her again. "To you."

Sammi sucked in a sharp breath. A sudden weakness seized her. She didn't know whether to throw herself at him or run for her life. The latter seemed infinitely safer. "You're right," she said, her voice barely audible. "It's time to remind you," *and me,* "that we're only friends and business associates."

Nick grinned wryly. "I'm aware of that. I just thought I should warn you. That dress, with you in it, is lethal, lady. In fact, what you have on now is . . ." He shook his head. "Sorry. Never mind. Are you hungry? I'm starved. Let's eat and you can tell me what you saw at the convention today."

Squelching the urge to run, Sammi took a deep breath. She had to regain control — of herself, of the situation. Nick was her boss, yet he claimed to be attracted to her. He'd even made a pass at her. She had no business having dinner with him.

On the other hand, what could happen in a public place? She could satisfy her craving for his company while still keeping him at arm's length. Yes. That sounded workable. As long as she kept things casual and didn't let him make any further remarks like the ones about the dress she just bought, dinner with Nick should be harmless enough.

She let her breath out slowly. "I have reservations at Trader Vic's. You're welcome to join me. I'll run up and put this," she rustled her shopping bag, "in my room and meet you at the restaurant."

Nick took the package from her hands. "No need for you to go all that way. We'll just drop this off with the bell captain and pick it up after we finish."

Since no sound argument came to mind, Sammi agreed.

On their way through the lobby, Nick caught the desk clerk staring at Sammi with something considerably more than polite interest. Nick ground his teeth and shot the man a glare most people would have backed away from. The clerk, damn him, didn't even notice.

"What's wrong?" Sammi asked. "You look like you're ready to murder someone."

Nick shook his head and laughed at himself. Surely that wasn't jealousy he felt. "Nothing. Just hungrier than I thought, I guess."

Amid Trader Vic's atmosphere of quality, elegance, and soothing, exotic Polynesian decor, Nick couldn't take his eyes off Sammi. When she talked about the exhibits in the convention hall, her face lit up with enthusiasm.

"And the deburring machine J. W. wanted me to look at—Nick you wouldn't believe the one I saw. It's almost as big as the new CNC Router. It holds the parts in place with bottom suction while it deburs the top, then the parts slide into the other half, with suction on the top side to hold them in place while the underneath is smoothed. It's fantastic!"

Nick grinned at her. "Did you get information on it to take back to J. W.?"

Sammi laughed. "You should see my hotel room."

No, Nick thought with a shudder, he shouldn't see her hotel room. He shouldn't see her anyplace where there was a bed.

"I picked up tons of brochures on everything. The airline will probably charge me extra to carry it all home. I may have to buy another suitcase just to pack it in."

"Forget the flight. You're coming with me."

"What do you mean? How are you getting home? Surely you didn't drive."

Nick leaned back in his chair in anticipation. "Are you forgetting what Elliott Air used to manufacture?"

It didn't take her more than a heartbeat to figure out what he meant. "You mean . . . you flew the Skybird? And I'm going back with you?"

He grinned again. She looked like a kid waiting for Santa. "If that's all right with you," he said with mock seriousness.

"All right? Nick, I can hardly wait!"

All day Tuesday, Wednesday, and Thursday, Nick and Sammi walked the convention floor, sometimes together, sometimes splitting off in different directions. They viewed the latest machinery and tools, the very best technology the world had to offer for the manufacturing industry. They attended workshops, seminars and speeches.

And every time she and Nick separated, Sammi wondered why he had really come to Chicago. Because when they were together, he seemed to spend more time watching her than looking at the exhibits. The scary thing was, she liked having him look at her. Reveled in it. Under his gaze she felt feminine, powerful . . . beautiful. Things she hadn't felt with any degree of confidence in a long time.

Yet she was the one who had put limits on their relationship, and her reasons were still valid. She might look different, with her new makeup and hairstyle. She might feel different about herself. But she was still the same Sammi she had always been. The one who couldn't hold her own husband's interest.

Jim had not been half the man Nick was. If she couldn't hold Jim, she had no hope at all of keeping Nick's interest. Not for long. And she had no desire for a fling. There was still her job to consider, and the work that made her feel good about herself. It paid better than any other she could hope to get.

So she would just have to learn to live with wanting, and not having, Nick Elliott.

It was with considerable pride that she realized, during those three days with Nick in Chicago, that she could be his friend and enjoy his company without giving away her secret longings. But when she forgot herself and touched his hand or held his arm, it became harder each time to let go.

Finally it was Friday and time to leave. Sammi breathed a sigh of relief. She was so excited about flying home in the Skybird 2000, she would undoubtedly make a fool of herself before a seasoned pilot like Nick. But better a fool out of herself over flying than one out of herself over Nick.

At eight-fifteen, Sammi, Nick, and Mark Heywood piled into a cab for the ride to Midway. As she had done since leaving home, Sammi had left her hair hanging loose rather than twisted into its usual knot. She told herself she left it that way because it was more comfortable. Surely her reason had nothing to do with the way Nick's gaze clung to the swaying curls.

And surely she hadn't dressed this morning in

a pair of snug black slacks and a cowl-necked sweater whose powder-blue color flattered her skin just because she thought Nick would like them. Surely not.

Nick had undoubtedly not given her a thought when he dressed this morning in faded, hip-hugging denims and a tailored, long-sleeved white shirt. He certainly had no idea how the crisp whiteness set off his tan and affected her breathing. She and Nick were just friends, after all. How could he know of her breathing problems? How could he know what the sight of his muscular forearms below his rolled-up sleeves, or the glimpse of dark chest hair through his open collar, did to her pulse?

He couldn't know. She didn't want him to. They were, after all, just friends.

When they reached Midway Airport, Sammi concentrated on her surroundings to take her mind off Nick. It worked. She got so caught up in looking at all the planes, she nearly missed spotting the 2000. Then she saw it and gasped. The shiny white Skybird sparkled in the sun. *Come,* it called to Sammi. *Fly me, fly me.*

"Oh, Nick, isn't it beautiful?"

"Yes, very."

She followed Nick out of the cab, and he nudged her toward the plane. Sammi stood her ground and simply stared at the sleek, powerful-looking craft.

"Trust me," Nick said. "It's a lot easier to fly

from the inside. Come on." He took her by the hand and tugged her on board.

The inside of the Skybird was every bit as splendid as the outside, with a plush, rich interior Sammi hadn't expected. She sat next to a window in a chair that looked and felt more like an expensive living room recliner than an airplane seat. Soft crushed velvet caressed her and hugged to her shape. Sheer comfort, done in restful mauve and beige. The armrests and even the seat belts were padded and covered in matching fabric.

Sammi sat back and sighed. "This is heaven."

"Not yet." Nick took the seat next to her and smiled. "But we're headed in that general direction."

Soon the engine revved and so did Sammi's heart. They taxied forward, and it seemed like an eternity before they finally started speeding down the runway.

Sammi gripped Nick's hand. At lift-off, her stomach jumped up to her chest. She laughed at the sensation. The higher they climbed, the tighter she gripped Nick's hand. Not in fear, but in excitement. She laughed again when she felt the landing gear thump up into place.

"Oh, Nick." She turned to face him. "Thank you for this." Strictly on impulse, she leaned over and kissed his cheek.

Before she could pull away, Nick captured the back of her head in his palm. There it was again, that look of heat and fire in his eyes.

Then he whispered close to her lips, "Do that again."

Sammi swallowed, feeling the urge to comply well up inside. "I . . . I shouldn't."

His gaze roamed her face, coming back time and again to her lips, her eyes. "No," he finally said. "You shouldn't. Neither should I." But he leaned closer until, if she moved but a fraction of an inch, their mouths would touch.

Sammi's heart raced to a new rhythm, hard and fast and undeniably strong. "This is crazy."

"Yes."

"We can't get involved."

"I know." His fingers massaged her scalp. "I love your hair down this way."

Sammi closed her eyes. God, what was he doing to her? Why was she fighting it?

Then she remembered all her own arguments. They were still true, still valid. What she felt right then was probably just the excitement of the flight, nothing more. It couldn't be more.

She opened her eyes and looked at him, her heart breaking a little with each word she spoke. "Nick, we can't do this."

He eased his hold on her head and ran his fingers through the length of her hair. "We can if you say we can."

"No," she said. "We can't."

She pulled away, and he let her go.

Sammi spent several minutes staring out the

window at a sky so blue it hurt to look at it before realizing she still held Nick's hand. Reluctantly, and with more willpower than she knew she possessed, she unthreaded her fingers from his and clutched her hands together in her lap.

Ten

In the weeks following Sammi and Nick's return from Chicago, the paperwork went through on the Theodolite System. The loan was in place, and the equipment scheduled to be installed next month. Meanwhile, Sammi buried herself in her latest project, the feasibility study regarding Elliott Air's possible resumption of aircraft manufacturing.

Nick knew what she was doing, and he wished her luck. But he doubted she would find her proposed venture profitable enough for the company to undertake, no matter how badly he wanted it to be otherwise.

God, to be able to build planes again. It was a dream he hadn't shared with anyone in years. Not since Sam Barnett. Not since the Maverick. Thanks to Barnett, the Maverick, the craft Nick had designed and tested and would have given his life for, was forever out of his reach.

Damn that Barnett. If the man hadn't conveniently died in an auto accident two years ago, Nick would be sorely tempted to murder him.

But remembering how the double-dealing Barnett had cheated him did no good. All the memories served to accomplish was to noticeably raise Nick's blood pressure. He forced himself to take several deep breaths and think of something calm. Sammi.

Wrong image. Thinking of Sammi was anything but calming. The minute they had returned from Chicago she had slipped back into her camouflage again. At least now, however, she occasionally wore her hair down. That, too, did nothing to soothe him, only made him want to take in handfuls of the wild auburn curls and wind all that glorious hair around his hands until he held her face close to his and . . .

Damn.

He had to face facts. She wasn't the least interested in him. Not as a man, anyway. All she seemed to want these days was his agreement to accompany her to New Orleans for the National Business Aircraft Association's annual convention.

She came at him again later that afternoon.

"Come on, Nick, you know you want to go."

"Damn it, Sammi, it's just not practical. Even if you did convince me to start building the Skybird again, what does the NBAA have to do with anything? That's strictly for business aircraft. The 2000 can't compete in that market.

The plane's not big enough for most corporate use."

"So maybe I'm trying to keep from putting all our eggs in one basket. Did you ever think of that?"

Nick rolled his eyes. *Eggs in a basket?* "You really are a farm girl, aren't you?"

"You're missing the point. On purpose, I think. What I don't understand is why? You usually have an open, except on this issue."

"I haven't closed my mind. You just haven't convinced me the idea won't send this whole company straight down the tubes, permanently this time."

"That's why I want you to go to New Orleans. To help convince you."

Nick's phone rang. *Saved by the bell.* Trite, but true, Nick thought. The lure to give in to Sammi was so great he didn't trust his judgment any longer. She couldn't be right. It wasn't feasible to start building planes again. Because he wanted it too badly, and when Nick wanted something that badly, with his heart and soul, it usually fell apart in his hands. Like the Maverick, like . . .

"Sorry," he told Sammi. "My three o'clock appointment is here. We'll have to finish this discussion later."

As far as Sammi was concerned, Nick seemed just a little too relieved to end their meeting. She knew he wanted to build planes. She had

186

seen the look in his eyes that day in the conference room. Why wouldn't he give her a chance to convince him?

"We'll finish it, all right," she muttered to herself as she left his office. "But that won't be until he agrees to go to New Orleans with me."

She went back to her research. Late that afternoon Henry called and asked how things were going.

"Okay, I guess," she said. "If you don't count that the company president is stubborn as a mule."

"What about this time?"

"I'm trying to talk him into going to the NBAA with me at the end of the month."

There was a pause before Henry asked, "Why the NBAA?"

"It has to do with a new project of mine," she hedged.

"Anything to do with trying to convince him to start building planes again?"

"He told you that?"

"He mentioned it. Am I right?"

Sammi sighed. "Yes, for all the good I'm doing. I can tell he wants it, Henry. But he won't give me the chance to prove we can do it. I'd like to tie him to his chair so he can't get away while I have my say."

Henry chuckled. "You just keep after him. You can be pretty persuasive when you try. Believe me, I know."

When Sammi and Henry said good-bye a few minutes later, Sammi returned to her research. It was some time before she found what she was looking for.

"This is it!" There *was* a large hole in the market for business aircraft. One she knew Elliott Air could fill.

She had to talk to Nick. She jumped up from her desk and took off down the hall. She was almost to Nick's office before she felt the cold tile through her hose. She stopped and looked down. For heaven's sake, she'd forgotten her shoes.

Embarrassed, she headed back to her office, peering around, hoping no one would see her barefoot. But no one was around. Not a soul. And it was so quiet she could hear the fluorescent lights hum overhead.

She looked at her watch. "Well, damn." It was six-thirty. Nick, and everyone else, was long gone. No wonder the offices were so quiet. In frustration, she carted stacks of reports home with her, determined to arm herself thoroughly and confront him again tomorrow. He simply had to attend the NBAA.

When she walked into her apartment, her phone was ringing. It was Henry.

"He's not tied," Henry said, "but he looks pretty darned comfortable in that chair in my den. You want him, come at him. I'll hold him down, but you have to do the convincing."

188

Sammi dropped her pile of paperwork onto the couch. "Are you talking about Nick?"

"Who else?"

That breathless feeling came back. "I'll be right there." She told herself, as she had for several weeks, that the fluttering in her chest was merely the result of her excitement over pursuing her pet project. But deep down, she knew it was the thought of seeing Nick, even though she saw him every day.

Maybe going to New Orleans with him wouldn't be such a good idea, if she couldn't control her reactions to the mere thought of him any better than this.

But no, he had to go with her to New Orleans. She would simply not give in to the feelings he stirred in her.

By the time she reached Henry's she had once again convinced herself she could learn to ignore her growing attraction to Nick Elliott.

"Well, look who's here!"

Henry's booming announcement jarred the peace and quiet of the den. Whatever ease Nick had found, slight though it may have been, evaporated with the tightening of his shoulders. He was going to have to open his eyes. Henry obviously had company. Nick braced himself to stand.

"No, no, don't get up," Henry said. "In fact,

have another drink. Sammi, can I get you anything?"

Nick's head snapped up.

"No, thank you," she told Henry.

What the devil was she doing there? Nick had almost managed to get his mind off her for a short time.

If she had been home since leaving work, she hadn't bothered to change clothes, for she still wore the gray suit he hated more than anything he had yet seen her wear. The skirt and jacket were loose, shapeless, and large enough to hide every curve of her body. Camouflage.

The sight should have left him disinterested, but Nick wasn't that lucky. The formless clothing teased him with mere hints of the body he knew lay beneath and brought sharp images to mind of Sammi in her sleek black swimsuit. He felt his shoulders—among other certain body parts—tighten.

The clink of ice cubes hitting glass tensed Nick's shoulders even more. Henry took the empty glass from Nick's hand and replaced it with a fresh scotch and water.

"Have at him, girl," Henry said. "He's all yours."

Nick glanced from one to the other. "I think I've been set up."

"Now, Nick—"

"You stay out of this," Nick warned Henry. "Sammi, I swear, if this is about the NBAA—"

"Yes, it is. Just hear me out, Nick, from start to finish, for once. Please?"

Please. Damn. He sat back in his chair. "All right, give me your best shot. But don't expect me to change my mind." He couldn't. He just couldn't give in and make that out-of-town trip with Sammi. Not only did he feel it would be a waste of company time and money, but he didn't trust himself, or her, alone together on another trip. If he had pressed her in Chicago, she might have given in to him. Her resistance was weakening. He didn't trust himself not to push for a more intimate relationship if they traveled together again.

Hell, he barely trusted himself not to throw her on the floor right there in front of Henry.

He gripped his glass tightly and took a long drink.

Sammi gave him a mock frown, then started pacing back and forth in front of him, her mind obviously on business.

Nick's mind was on the length of golden legs below the knee-length hem of her skirt.

"Let's talk business jets," Sammi said.

Nick looked at Henry, who shrugged, as if to say, "I don't know where she's headed with this."

"Today's newest models are built on yesterday's designs, which were built on designs from the day before. Aircraft manufacturers traditionally look at their current model and say, 'How

191

can we make it bigger, better, faster?' " She stopped pacing and whirled toward Nick. "Right?"

Nick set his drink down and crossed his arms. "I suppose."

Sammi frowned. "Right." She started pacing again. "So every new model that comes along for the business jet market is bigger and better and faster than its predecessor. And more expensive. So when was the last time anybody started completely from scratch and designed a plane using all the modern technology available right from the start, when creating the actual design, rather than changing an existing model into something new?"

Nick sat up straighter. He shot Henry a look. "What have you been telling her?"

"Nothing," Henry said, "I swear."

"What could Henry have told me?"

"Never mind," Nick said. He sat back again. She wasn't talking about the Maverick. The Maverick was dead. As dead as Sam Barnett.

"Go on," Nick said to Sammi.

She gave him a long, studied look, then started pacing again. "When was the last time a company tried to produce a *less* expensive model than what's on the market?"

The tightness in Nick's shoulders spread to his neck.

"Still fast," Sammi said, "still comfortable—you bigwig executive types do like your comfort—but smaller maybe than most business jets. Say, a six-placer. Smaller and less expensive, yet with all the advanced technology available."

Nick rolled his head. She was about five years too late with her idea. He hated to burst her bubble—she looked so damned alive when excitement lit her eyes and colored her cheeks. Her every movement was sharp and sure and so full of vibrant energy. But she had to realize her idea wasn't unique. "I'll tell you when," he said. "Right now. You're describing the Swearingen SJ30 and Cessna's new CitationJet."

"Very good." Sammi gave him a mock curtsey. "Two points for you. But Nick, think. That's only two models for the entire corporate world to choose from when they want a smaller business jet. Two. And when they're actually on the market, the SJ30 will go for over two and a half million, the CitationJet for nearly three million. Cheap compared to their nearest competitor, yes. But we could come in under that."

"Under two and a half million for a fast, comfortable six-passenger business jet? You didn't forget to add in the engines, did you?"

Sammi plopped her hands on her hips. "Give me some credit. First, we're smaller than Swearingen and Cessna, so we don't have the overhead they do, but we still have the resources. Barnett was on the verge of doing this very thing several years ago."

At the mention of Barnett's name, Nick tensed even more.

"Imagine," Sammi said shaking her head. "Six months from FAA certification on his new Maverick, and he died in a car crash."

Nick ground his teeth and glared at Henry.

Henry once again shrugged and shook his head.

"It's a shame nobody's been able to contact the heirs about buying the design. The Maverick would be perfect for us to build. With a little updating, of course."

"What updating?" Nick demanded. "You said it yourself, the Maverick was perfect, or as near perfect as a plane can get."

"Yes, but that was several years ago. By now the cost of producing it will have gone up too much to get in under the two and a half million mark. But we could knock the price down some with panel-mounted avionics instead of remote-mounted."

"By God, listen to her," Henry cried. "She sounds like she's been building planes all her life."

Sammi smiled at Henry. "Why thank you, sir, but it's just good research, that's all."

It was damn good, but Nick kept the thought to himself. She was riding high enough already. He didn't intend to let it go to her head. "Nice thought, but the Maverick is beyond our reach. Anyway, I thought you wanted us to resume production of the 2000."

"I do, but I'm looking to the future. Besides, we can't start up with the 2000 again until that Product Liability Bill passes. If anyone in this blasted industry knew who Barnett's designer was, we could hire him. But since the mystery man seems to have vanished, we'll just have to find someone else, or do it ourselves. I've heard you've dabbled in that area," she said to Nick.

"Dabbled," Henry said. "Now there's a good word."

Nick shot him a narrowed look. "Don't you have something better to do than hang around here?"

Henry grinned. "I suppose I could find something." He tossed Sammi a wink. "This means he's about to give in, but doesn't want any witnesses. Have at him, girl."

With Henry's footsteps fading down the hallway, Nick turned back to Sammi. "So what does any of this have to do with New Orleans?"

"Because that's where we can learn if anyone else is getting ready to join the game. The first company to produce a small business jet that comes in under the SJ30 and the CitationJet will be able to grab a sizeable chunk of the market, providing they get in soon enough. But the latecomers will be just that—late. Before we can make a decision or any plans, we have to know who is planning what that might affect us."

"That doesn't mean I have to go," Nick said.

"Damn it, Nick," she cried. She braced her hands on the arms of his chair and leaned over him. Her hair fell forward and brushed his cheeks. Her scent clouded his brain. Her lips, and that damn mole, teased with their closeness. The fire of conviction in her eyes acted like an aphrodisiac on his already eager libido.

"Nick," she said, her brown eyes capturing his gaze. "I need you there. I can't cover the whole convention thoroughly on my own. And you know these people, I don't. They'll tell you things they won't tell me. You can ask questions I couldn't get away with. Say you'll go with me, Nick. Say it."

Nick felt a sinking sensation in the pit of his stomach. She was right, she did need him at the convention. But he wanted her to need him in her life.

He didn't trust his own judgment where she was concerned. Was he thinking of giving in for the sake of the company, or for his own selfish wants?

She leaned closer until her breath fanned his lips. "Say it, Nick."

Say it quick so she'll back away.

"All right, I'll go. But I shouldn't."

"Why not?"

She didn't back away. His control snapped. "Because of this, damn it." He grasped her arms and tugged.

196

Sammi felt herself falling into his deep blue eyes . . . and onto his lap! Her cry of surprise got lost somewhere between his lips and hers as their mouths met.

Yes! she thought. *Yes, Nick, yes.* This once there would be no denial, no listening to common sense, no worry about the future. This time she would let him kiss her, and she would kiss him back. Just this once.

She wrapped her arms around his neck. She felt his pause of surprise, then his moan of agreement. His arms came around her back and pulled her flush against his chest.

He wanted her. She couldn't deny it any longer, any more than she could deny wanting him. His hunger was fierce and hot and all for her. She knew it suddenly in her heart. She felt it in the way his tongue caressed hers, the way his hands roamed feverishly across her back, the way he hardened beneath her hip.

A burning ache throbbed deep inside her. She squeezed her eyes shut to hold it all in and lost herself to the magic of his mouth and hands, the wildness he set loose in her, the heat he burned her with. She, who towered over so many people, felt small and vulnerable in his arms. Yet at the same time she felt powerful, as if she could conquer the world, as long as Nick held her.

Nick eased his fierce hold on her and pulled back.

She didn't want to let him go, but she knew she had no business holding him, kissing him, sitting on his lap.

When his lips left hers, she ached for more, but knew it couldn't be. She opened her eyes and found him watching her.

"Well, well," Henry said from the doorway.

Sammi jerked and blushed.

"Get lost, Henry," Nick said. His blue eyes still held Sammi captive.

"I'm gone."

Sammi knew when Henry left the room again—his laughter trailed down the hall to the kitchen. She started to rest her head against Nick's shoulder. She needed a moment to catch her breath and let the world stop spinning.

But Nick stopped her with a hand on her cheek. "Sammi," he whispered roughly. "I can't promise this won't happen again. I can't keep lying to you, to myself."

Her body tingled in answer, but what verbal answer could she give him? Could she say it was all right, she understood, she agreed? Those things were true, yet she could not bring herself to admit them out loud.

"Do you still want me to go to New Orleans with you?"

Sammi lowered her gaze. "Yes, but . . ."

"But, no strings? No promises? No pressure from me for more?"

She gave him a half-smile. "Something like

198

that."

He ran a calloused thumb over her cheek. "I'll do my best, Samantha."

The way he said her name, full out, soft and low, turned her bones to jelly. If he said another word, she might just burst into tears. "I . . . I'd better go." With all the grace of a charm school dropout, she climbed from his lap. "Tell Henry good night."

Without looking back, she picked up her briefcase and left. She made it halfway home before the tears started.

"What am I going to do?" she cried.

Nick stared across the empty room, Sammi's fragrance still clinging to his hands and shirt.

"Do you know what you're doing?"

Henry's voice startled him. Nick got up and refilled his drink. He was definitely putting a dent in Henry's supply of Chevas tonight. "Does any man know what he's doing when it comes to a woman?"

Henry poured himself two fingers of Jack Daniel's. "Good point. But Sammi's not any woman. You just don't hurt her, you hear?"

"I'm doing my best not to." *I just don't know if my best is good enough.*

Nick eyed Henry's drink. "Should you be doing that after a heart attack?"

Henry waved the words away. "Don't worry about it. Why didn't you tell Sammi about the Maverick?" Henry asked.

"Why should I? It's dead, just like Sam Barnett."

When Henry didn't answer, Nick turned and looked at him. Henry simply stared, his head cocked to one side. Then the man shook his head. "If you say so. You ought to know."

"I don't want you saying anything to Sammi."

"Me?"

"I mean it."

Henry just smiled. "Anything you say, Nick."

Now why, Nick wondered, did he have the feeling the old man had something up his sleeve?

Eleven

During the week and a half remaining before the New Orleans convention, Sammi managed most of the time to avoid so much as being in the same room with Nick. When that wasn't possible, she made certain they were at least never alone together.

The effort was exhausting. It was also woefully inadequate as a means to keep her mind off Nick. She was so preoccupied with thoughts of him she nearly missed another staff meeting. If she hadn't whacked her elbow on the edge of her desk, dropped her pencil into the wastebasket, then had to fish it out, she might never have noticed the memo beneath the empty orange juice carton.

Juice? She hadn't had any in the office in days.

Sammi picked up the phone and called Darla. "Have you noticed anyone in my office today?"

"Not that I can think of. Why?"

"I just . . . thought someone might have

201

brought me some papers or been looking for me."

"The only one I can think of is me, when I put a memo on your desk."

"Oh. Okay. Thanks, Darla."

Still puzzled over the orange juice carton, Sammi picked up her notes and headed for the meeting. She supposed it wasn't all that unusual for someone to stop in her office while she wasn't there and toss something into her wastebasket.

As for the memo, in her current state of preoccupation over a certain man, Sammi could easily have knocked the memo into the trash first thing this morning when she had shoved things out of the way to make room for her briefcase.

Lord, she had to get her mind back on her job. She was supposed to be impressing Nick with her competence, and instead, she felt like she was about to fly apart at the seams.

What she needed were at least fifty laps in the nearest pool.

The staff meeting was an hour of sheer torture. Every time she made the mistake of looking at Nick she remembered the feel of his arms around her, the touch of his hands, the taste of his lips, and all the tingling, giddy emotions those things had made her feel.

The instant the meeting was over, Sammi fled back to her office.

Nick watched her hustle out the door of the conference room as if her skirt were on fire. He was quite possibly making the biggest mistake of his life in going to New Orleans with her. His hunger for her grew daily and gnawed at his insides. He was becoming obsessed with Sammi Carmichael.

The hardest thing for him to forget was the way she had come alive in his arms the last time he had kissed her. She hadn't pulled away, hadn't said no. She had met him kiss for kiss and stunned him with the passion he had always known she had.

And now the two of them were traveling out of town together, and he was supposed to keep his distance? He wasn't sure he was that strong.

Yet somehow, by the next Monday when they boarded their commercial flight to New Orleans, Nick decided that, with a little cooperation from Sammi, he could control himself.

He thought that all during the fifty-minute flight to their Dallas-Fort Worth stopover, during the rush to catch their connecting flight, and all the way through takeoff of that last leg of the trip. Right up until Sammi fell asleep beside him and her head rolled over against his shoulder.

That was his first indication of the seriousness of his situation.

Nick had had kind thoughts, warm, caring thoughts about certain women in his past. Intimate thoughts, hot thoughts, even hungry thoughts. But he had never felt this fierce, primal urge to protect and cherish that overwhelmed him at the feel of her head resting trustingly against his shoulder.

He squeezed his eyes shut and tried to concentrate on the drone of the engines. It didn't work.

God help him, he was in love with her.

Their flight landed at New Orleans International Airport just past noon, and Nick and Sammi took a cab to the Marriott. The Hilton Riverside was the official hotel for the convention, but Nick had waited so late to agree to attend, the Hilton had been booked solid. No wonder, with more than sixteen thousand attendees expected. But Sammi didn't care where they stayed. She was just grateful Nick had come with her.

Under a clear blue sky, she drank in all the sights during the cab ride. She marveled at the above-ground cemetery, the modern Superdome, and all the beautiful old buildings. Such history!

Nick must have noticed her interest in their surroundings, for he suggested they do some sightseeing as soon as they checked in at the Marriott. "Once the convention opens in the morning—"

"We won't have any spare time," Sammi finished for him.

"Right. So what do you say to playing tourist?"

"Yes!"

For Sammi, the afternoon was magical. With Nick leading the way, they strolled the riverwalk, toured the aquarium, visited Lafayette Square, rode the St. Charles street car through the lovely antebellum neighborhoods, saw Loyola and Tulane Universities and Audubon Park, and still made it to the French Quarter before the shops closed. Sammi's head was practically spinning from cramming so much activity into one afternoon.

In the French Quarter, Nick insisted Sammi try a cup of chicory coffee, but she much preferred the chewy praline that followed.

There was so much to take in, Sammi wished she could spend a month without leaving the Vieux Carré . . . A month with Nick at her side, watching her, laughing with her, encouraging her enthusiasm. She felt as though she were the center of his world, and it was a heady feeling.

For dinner they ate corn dogs on the curb across the street from Jackson Square and the St. Louis Cathedral while watching a clown make funny animals out of balloons.

So many sights, so many scents and sounds. All of New Orleans swirled in Sammi's head that night, making sleep elusive. She sat at her hotel window and watched the Canal Street Ferry sweep across the river and back between huge barges, some headed upriver, some down.

It was the wee hours of the morning before she made herself crawl into bed and close her eyes. And there, behind her lids, against an everchanging backdrop of all she had seen that day, stood Nick, smiling, laughing, teasing her.

She managed less than three hours of sleep.

In the city known as the Big Easy, the National Business Aircraft Association convention was anything but. After the opening press conference Tuesday morning on the state of the industry, Sammi and Nick split up to cover more territory. Nick took on Lakefront Airport, where the planes were on static display. Sammi stayed at the convention center and visited as many as possible of the six hundred exhibits and the several dozen press conferences held by exhibitors announcing new and future projects.

She saw nearly every new engine on the market, from General Motors' Allison division to the new Garrett engines from Allied Signal, plus the latest developments from Pratt & Whitney Canada, TBM International, and Williams International, and picked up literature on many of them. She looked at the latest in avionics, full-scale cockpits, cabin mockups, and noise supressors to make older aircraft conform to new federal regulations. She spent nearly a half hour viewing the mockup of Swearingen's new SJ30. She eavesdropped on the Corporate Aviation Management Committee meeting and attended a special session by the FAA on Titanium Rotating Components.

By Thursday afternoon she was beyond exhaustion and knew Nick was, too. Yet Sammi also felt her optimism rising with each hour of the convention. She saw and heard nothing to indicate any other company besides Swearingen and Cessna had plans for a low-cost business jet. In fact, the opposite was true. Many of the conversations she overheard were of making future models bigger and fancier, which also translated to costlier.

In addition to her rising optimism, something else stirred inside Sammi during those three hectic days, something warm and fluttery one minute, hot and shivery the next, that grew stronger each time she saw Nick, each time he looked at her through hooded eyes. His words may have been all business, he may have refrained from so much as a simple touch, but his eyes . . . ah, the things that man could say with those blue eyes.

They revealed his own growing excitement over the possibility of Sammi's proposed project. They also showed other things, blatantly.

His eyes said, *You're beautiful.* And she felt so.

They said, *I want to hold you, kiss you,* and she wanted those things, too.

They said, *Remember? Remember when we kissed? I want to taste you again, but this time I don't want to stop.* And that fluttery, shivery something shot through her blood. It was called anticipation. And it terrified her.

She and Nick agreed they would attend the Thursday night Awards Banquet, so Sammi slipped out of the convention a couple of hours early for a much-needed nap and a stern talking-to. She simply had to stop these feelings for Nick. She had to.

That decision made, she undressed and stretched out in bed. To be safe, she requested a wakeup call so she wouldn't sleep through the Awards Banquet. She needn't have worried, for she didn't sleep at all. The minute her head touched the pillow she was wide awake and thinking of Nick.

When it was time to get ready to meet him in the lobby for the ride to the banquet at the Hilton, Sammi sat on the edge of the bed and stared at her clothes hanging in the closet. She reminded herself of her earlier resolve to get Nick off her mind.

But other thoughts tormented her. Was he really the type of man who would fire her if they had an affair and then ended it? What if she pushed him away one too many times, and he left her alone? Is that what she really wanted? What if she got that wish? She would then never know what it was like to make love with a man who set her blood on fire with just a look.

She stared at the neat array of hangars, thinking . . . thinking . . .

Nick was proud of himself. All they had left was one last night, and that they would spend with more than fifteen hundred people. They were safe. He and Sammi would be able to get on the plane in the morning and go home without having severely complicated their relationship. The tight feeling he'd been experiencing in his chest for more than a week began to ease.

When Sammi stepped out of the elevator a moment later, he realized the other tightening, lower down than his chest, wasn't about to ease. Not if she didn't do something drastic, like maybe smear mud on her face. He doubted even that would help. He caught himself straightening his tie.

He didn't know what he was getting so worked up about. Sammi was covered from neck to knees, shoulders to fingertips, in a blue fox coat. Upon closer inspection, he determined the fur was synthetic. He should have realized Sammi wouldn't turn loose of enough money to buy something so frivolous as the genuine article.

It wasn't her body, because he couldn't see it. Maybe it was that mile and a half of legs that turned him on. Or that wild tangle of hair that looked as if she had just crawled out of a man's bed.

Then he saw it, the reason his heart was suddenly pumping at high speed. It was the look in her eyes. A hot, sexy look, with just a touch of shyness. God, what he wouldn't give to know what she was thinking just then.

All week, and longer, Nick had avoided even the most casual physical contact with her. She had equally avoided him. But now he offered her his arm, and she took it, her eyes on him while she smiled.

He couldn't help it. He smiled back. "You look . . . sensational."

She lowered her eyes and her cheeks turned rosy. Then her lids rose slowly, deliberately, he would swear, until she looked him shyly in the eye. "So do you."

Her breathy whisper sent hot shivers down his spine.

It was a full hour before they were seated at their table at the NBAA Annual Awards Banquet. Nick thanked his lucky stars that Henri LeBlanc, a friend of his from the Aerospatiale home office in France, and Henri's wife Margot, were at the same table. Having friends to

210

talk with helped ease the electric tension that had increased between Nick and Sammi during the short cab ride from the Marriott to the nearby Hilton.

The LeBlancs sat on Sammi's left, while Nick sat to her right. He leaned toward her and performed the introductions. Then he said to Sammi, "It's plenty warm in here. Do you want me to check your coat?"

He could have sworn a flash of . . . what? Fear? . . . crossed her eyes. She licked her lips. "Uh, no, thanks. But I think I will take it off."

He meant to help her, but someone on his right nudged his shoulder. He turned and greeted Bob Walsh from Gulfstream's Georgia plant. When he turned back around to Sammi, he froze. His mind went blank and his mouth went dry. All he could do was stare at the soft turquoise silk and bare, golden shoulders.

Sammi felt his gaze on her like a living flame. Where he looked, she burned. She waited, breath held, for his reaction.

"What a stunning dress," Margot said.

Sammi turned gratefully, unable to bear the suspense. "Thank you," she answered.

"Did you get it here? You must tell me which shop."

"No, I, uh . . ." She glanced at Nick. His gaze darted down her dress and back up before he looked away. A muscle in his jaw twitched. "I got it in Chicago last month."

Margot turned and spoke to her husband. Sammi glanced at Nick again. At the blank look in his eyes, sheer terror gripped her.

For her ears alone, he asked, "Did you forget my warning?"

Sammi lowered her gaze and noticed Nick was gripping the edge of the table so hard his knuckles were white. She glanced back at his face. He was turned sideways in his chair, his body facing her but his head was turned away again. That muscle in his jaw ticked once, twice.

This was it, then. The moment of truth. "No," she told him, "I didn't forget."

He whipped his head around, shock plain on his face.

With her heart pounding clear up into her throat, Sammi tried to swallow. It didn't work. She glanced away from him. The deafening drone of hundreds of voices kept her words private. "That is, unless you've . . . changed your mind."

Still gripping the table, Nick turned toward her. "Not on your life, lady," he said softly. "As long as you really mean it."

With the relief that seemed to wilt her bones, Sammi felt a sharp new fear. Before this night was over, she and Nick were going to make love. She knew it, wanted it. Every cell in her body begged for it. But . . . what if she failed to please him? How would she ever face him again? How would she live with the disappointment?

Nick ran his fingers through his hair. "Do you, Sammi? Do you mean it?"

Something in his voice compelled her to face him. His hand trembled where it lay on the table. *He's as nervous as I am!* Her fear melted away "Yes, Nick, I really mean it."

The flare of heat in his eyes stirred an answering fire inside her.

The evening turned into the longest night of Sammi's life. The speeches and presentations seemed endless, and she didn't taste any of the food she ate, although she was certain it was some of the best in the country.

With every agonizingly long moment that dragged past, all Sammi could think was, *Soon, soon!*

But soon seemed to get farther away every minute.

Through it all, Nick barely took his eyes off her. His laughter grew sharper, his gaze darker, his eyes more hooded. When the banquet officially ended, Sammi thought, *Now.*

It wasn't to be. Henri and Margot insisted on buying Sammi and Nick a drink somewhere in the French Quarter. Try though he did—Sammi had to give him credit for that—Nick could not get out of the invitation gracefully. Henri simply refused to take no for an answer.

The look Nick gave Sammi took her breath

away. The apology in his blue eyes was nearly lost in the message of yearning and promise plainly visible. A yearning that matched her own. A promise of something hot and intimate. She shuddered.

Nick helped her slip her coat on. The delicious brush of his fingers against her bare shoulders nearly buckled her knees.

As they followed the other couple outside to a waiting cab, Sammi caught Nick glaring at Henri's back. She laughed. Nick shot her a look of pure frustration before finally laughing with her.

The driver held the car door open.

"Who's going to ride in the front?" Henri asked.

"Not me." Nick stepped forward and tugged Sammi in after him. "Excuse me," he said to Margot. He slid across the seat to the opposite door and pulled Sammi in next to him. Henri and Margot laughed and crowded into the back seat with them.

The driver let them out at the vehicle barricade on Bourbon Street. Even though it was eleven at night in the middle of the week, and the weather was chilly, the street was alive with light and crawling with people. People such as Sammi had never seen in her life.

This was a totally different atmosphere from the one Sammi and Nick had experienced in the daylight earlier in the week. By night Bourbon

Street became all neon and gaudy and fascinating—a whole new, wonderful, exciting world.

When Sammi stopped to gawk at the first head of green hair she'd ever seen, Nick roared with laughter. At her, not the hair.

She made a face at him. "So I've led a sheltered life. So what?"

"You are going to get an eyeful tonight, I promise."

The woman in the gold sequined evening gown walking toward them was at least as tall as Sammi, and was, in Sammi's opinion, a little on the showy side. Too much makeup. Odd, but the lady couldn't seem to make up her mind who to stare at hardest, Sammi, or Nick. When she drew closer Sammi gasped. "Oh my God!"

Nick turned Sammi abruptly away, his whole body shaking, and steered her across the street after Henri and Margot.

"Nick, did you see?"

"Hush," he said between laughs. "I saw, I saw."

"That was a *man*."

Nick leaned close until his forehead almost touched hers, his shoulders still shaking with laughter. "Keep your voice down. You'll hurt his feelings."

Henri and Margot hustled them from one overpacked smoke-filled nightclub to another. Henri promised they would have only one drink.

He just hadn't found the proper place yet.

After the third nightclub, Nick leaned toward Sammi again so she could hear him over the music blasting from the open doorway beside them. "Having a good time?"

She grinned up at him. "This is terrific—better than a county fair!"

At the next club, Henri spread his arms wide. *"Oui!* This is the place. Here we shall have our drink."

The club was packed with hot jazz, cold drinks, and a wall-to-wall crush of people of all types. Strange people, not-so-strange people, plain people, fancy people. But the person Sammi was most aware of was Nick.

The hostess showed the foursome to a small round table near the crowded dance floor. It was also near the small stage where the jazz band performed, so conversation was close to impossible.

After a round of drinks arrived at the table, the band changed direction. "A special request for all you lovers out there. Something slow and sexy. A little blues to hold your baby by."

Nick's eyes turned dark. "Dance with me?"

With those few words, the tension that had eased between them since leaving the banquet came slamming back. The fascination, the anticipation, the excitement. And for Sammi, a giddy case of nerves. But it never crossed her mind to deny his request. She rose and slipped off her coat.

She stepped with Nick onto the tiny, crowded dance floor. His hand rode the small of her back as he led them into the center of the floor, until they were hidden from view by the sheer crush of bodies. The heat from his touch seeped clear into her bones.

Starting with the low wail of a saxophone that was soon joined by a throbbing bass, the music was just as promised—slow and sexy. Sammi turned to Nick.

Nick let out a slow breath. Finally, he could hold her in his arms without worrying about who saw them. He took her hands and placed them behind his neck. The touch of her cool fingers inside his collar made his heart race.

Patience, he cautioned himself.

He wrapped his arms around her and pulled her close. The fit of their bodies was as he had known it would be—perfect.

"I wish," he said, looking into her eyes, "you hadn't taken off your coat."

"Why?"

Her breathy whisper, with her lips so close to his, sent a shiver down his spine. "Because then I could put my hands where I've been dying to put them all night, and no one could see."

Her eyes widened, her lips parted.

"But then," he said into her ear, "if you had your coat on, I wouldn't be able to—" He kissed her shoulder. "—kiss this pale streak—"

He nibbled the spot again and was rewarded when she shuddered against him. "—where your swimsuit goes."

He raised his head and looked into her eyes. And nearly groaned. "Do you have any idea what you do to me when you look at me like that?"

Sammi licked her lips. "Like what?"

He ran a hand up and down the silky back of her dress. "Like if I say or do the wrong—or right—thing, you'll melt right in my arms."

Her eyes turned dark.

Nick's heart slammed against his ribs. "Lord, what you do to me."

"What . . . do I do?"

He pulled her right hand from behind his neck and pressed it over his thundering heart. "This," he said. "Feel it. Feel what you do to me here." Then he pulled her hips flush against his. "And here."

Nick closed his eyes and savored the way she arched into him, putting the pressure of her abdomen right where he craved it. He rested his cheek against her head. The soft floral scent of her hair seeped into his brain and clouded his mind. He pressed his hips against hers again.

"Nick."

Her breath tickled his jaw. He pulled back and looked at her, suddenly sure he'd gone too far, certain that old look of caution would be back in her eyes.

But it wasn't. Instead of caution, he saw heat and hunger wild enough to match his own. The look nearly did him in. He raked a thumbnail down the zipper in the back of her dress. "Let's get out of here."

Her fingernails dug into his neck. Whether in agreement or protest, he didn't know, until she leaned and whispered in his ear, "Yes."

He didn't want to let go of her long enough to get off the dance floor, but knew if they stayed amid the crush of bodies and swayed chest to breast, hips to hips, to the throbbing rhythm of the blues for one more minute, he might very well shock and embarrass them both.

With one more quick hug and a hard, fast kiss, Nick let go of her and guided her back to their table. He wasn't sure what excuses he gave to Henri and Margot for breaking up the party, and he didn't care. He only knew it seemed like hours between the time he and Sammi left the dance floor until they stepped off the elevator and walked side by side to the door of her hotel room without touching. God, he didn't dare until they had privacy.

As Sammi pushed open the door to her room and stepped inside, Nick braced his hands on the jamb and took a deep breath. If his heart pounded any harder, it would surely pound its way right out of his chest.

Her room looked identical to his across the hall. He barely spared a glance at the elegant furnishings and plush carpet. He did notice she had a view of the river, which his room lacked, but it hardly mattered to him.

What did though was Sammi, and the way the bedside lamp, which she or the maid had left on, glittered in Sammi's auburn hair; the way she hugged herself as if she were cold; the way she stopped a few feet into the room and turned back toward him looking uncertain. "Nick?"

He took another deep breath. "Are you inviting me in?"

Her chest rose and fell beneath the blue fox. "Yes," she whispered.

Nick felt his gut tighten. "I won't leave, Samantha. You know what's going to happen. Are you still inviting me in?"

Twelve

Sammi swallowed hard. The look in his eyes scorched her with its heat. Yes, she knew what was going to happen, what she wanted.

She dropped her purse, then shrugged her coat from her shoulders and let it fall to the floor. "I'm still inviting you in."

With slow, deliberate movements, his hot blue gaze holding hers captive, he stepped into the room and pushed the door closed behind him. The click of the lock echoed in the stillness.

A sudden trembling seized Sammi, and along with it, doubts. Good heavens, what was she doing? She who had never been very good at intimacy was about to be as close with a man as a woman possibly could. A man of the world, a sophisticated man.

When his hands touched her bare shoulders she shivered.

"What's wrong?" he asked softly.

Suddenly she could no longer look him in the eye. She lowered her head.

"Sammi? Samantha?"

She squeezed her eyes shut. She wanted this. She *did*.

"What is it?"

"Nothing."

He squeezed her shoulders. "Then why are you shaking? Are you scared?"

Scared? Try terrified.

With a hand to her chin, he raised her head. "Look at me."

Sammi shook even harder. She had deliberately worn this dress, knowing exactly what he would think. That they were standing toe to toe in her hotel room was her doing. He was there at her invitation. She wanted him, hungered for him. The least she could do was look at him. She opened her eyes.

"You *are* scared."

"Not of you," she said quickly.

He pulled her closer to his heat. "Then what? What, Sammi?"

She couldn't look at him and say it, so she closed her eyes. "I've never been very . . . good at this. I'm afraid I'll . . . disappoint you."

He pulled her flush against him and wrapped his arms around her. "Ah, Samantha. Don't you know that's impossible? The only way you could come close to disappointing me is by asking me to leave."

His heat, his words, his arms holding her tight, sent warmth flooding through her. Like magic, her trembling stopped.

"Is that what you want?" Nick asked. "Do you want me to leave?"

"No!" She clutched at his back. "No."

He eased away slightly and looked at her. "Are you sure?"

With a hand on the back of his head, she brought his mouth toward hers. "Yes," she whispered. And with the word, she was sure. Being in Nick's arms was . . . right and necessary. It was as if everything in her life had pointed her in his direction. All of her past had guided her to this moment, this man. She brushed her lips on his. "Yes."

The pounding in Nick's chest hit double time. For one agonizing moment, he had feared she would send him away. But not now. Not now. She wanted him. Her eyes, her arms, her lips told him so. His knees shook with relief.

Then her lips touched his again. It was too much. And not enough. He tightened his hold on her and took her mouth in a kiss that surely told her of his fierce hunger, his wanting.

Her eager, willing response nearly cost him his control. He actually had his fists clenched in the turquoise silk, ready to rip it from her, before he realized what he was doing.

No. He didn't want to tear the dress. He didn't want the strength of his hunger to frighten her, and he damn sure didn't want anything to happen to the dress. He wanted to see her in it again and again. But not right now. Right now he wanted to see *her,* touch *her,* taste *her*.

With his mouth still devouring hers, he searched for her zipper and found it. It slid down without a hitch. Getting the dress off her while holding her so tight would be impossible, yet he didn't want to let her go, not for an instant. He spread his hands across her bare back and held her even tighter.

Then he groaned. Her entire back was bare. She wasn't wearing a bra. He should have realized, yet was glad he hadn't. The mere thought would have driven him crazy hours ago.

Still, as much as he craved the sight of her, he couldn't bring himself to let her go long enough to peel off the dress.

Then Sammi was pushing away from him, tearing at the front of his shirt. Her eagerness sent a tongue of fire licking at his loins. The sooner their clothes were gone, the sooner he would have her beneath him on the bed, and he could bury his aching flesh in her hot depths. A shudder ripped through him.

He eased back only far enough to help her remove his jacket and shirt, then he grasped the top of the turquoise silk and peeled it down her arms, baring her perfect, creamy breasts. Without his even touching them, her dark nipples puckered and hardened under his gaze. Another shudder took him.

Easy, easy. Slow down. Don't rush her.

Then she rushed him. She took a slow, deep breath and pushed her dress down her hips and thighs, revealing inch by agonizingly slow inch a lacy turquoise garter belt that nearly concealed the matching strip of panties beneath.

Nick sucked in a sharp breath. "Samantha . . ."

Her dress fell to the floor.

He didn't realize he was trembling until he saw how his fingers shook when he reached out to trace a strip of elastic that held up one sheer stocking.

Sammi barely felt his touch through the elastic strap, but it was enough to set her quivering. When he sank to his knees and pressed his face against her stomach, a hot tingling raced through her and settled between her thighs. She gripped his shoulders and hung on for dear life.

Then he released the garter belt snaps on one leg and peeled the stocking slowly down, following it with his lips. When he reached for the second set of snaps his knuckles brushed the front of her panties. "Nick . . ." Her knees buckled.

He caught her to him and wrapped her in his strong, warm arms. Her head spun, and the next she realized, she lay on the bed, and he covered her naked, aching body with his. God, the weight of him felt so right.

He shifted against her and she heard his shoes hit the floor. When he raised up on one arm to tug off his slacks, the loss of his weight chilled her. But when he covered her again, the heat of his bare skin, from chest to toes, branded her with its fire.

So many textures. She couldn't get enough of touching him. His hair-roughened legs against her smooth ones sent prickles of heat to her core. His shoulders and arms felt like contoured steel covered in satin. The thick silk of his hair brushed her cheek and made her breath catch.

Then he was kissing her again and she melted. His hands and lips touched her everywhere, setting her on fire and stealing her breath. When his hot mouth settled over the tip of one breast she squeezed her eyes shut to hold in the exquisite pleasure. Sheer emotion clogged her throat and radiated from her eyes.

He treated the other breast with equal attention, then trailed hot, moist kisses up her neck to her ear. Hot shivers raced down her arms.

Suddenly Nick stiffened and pulled back. "Sammi?"

Slowly, against her will, she opened her eyes.

"What is it?" he asked.

With her throat still seized up, she couldn't answer. She tried to reassure him with a smile, but that, too, was beyond her. All she could do was shake her head.

Nick cupped her face in his hands and used his thumbs to wipe the tears from beneath her eyes. His voice shook. "God, don't cry, Samantha, please don't cry. Tell me what's wrong."

Tears kept streaming from her eyes. "Nothing," she managed. "You just . . ."

His hands trembled against her face. "Just what? Tell me."

"You make me feel so . . . beautiful."

His eyes widened. "Samantha, you *are* beautiful. Don't you know that? Every living, breathing inch of you, inside and out. I —" He brushed his lips against hers, then sipped the remaining moisture from her cheeks. "You *are* beautiful."

A lover's words in the heat of passion, or did he really think her beautiful? Sammi didn't know, didn't care. Right then in his arms, with his blue eyes filled with intensity, she felt beautiful. She wrapped her arms around him and gave herself completely to the feelings he stirred in her.

A yawning emptiness throbbed deep inside her, an emptiness only Nick could fill.

Their kisses turned hot and urgent. His hands, steady now, found every sensitive spot on her body. Breathing heavily, he tore his lips from hers and settled them once again over the tip of one breast. After laving it lovingly, he drew back and blew on it. She watched him watch her nipple shrivel.

"So beautiful," he whispered.

Then he licked and sucked again until she squirmed beneath him. "Nick . . ."

He trailed a hand down her side and across her hip until he reached the juncture of her legs. As he touched the very center of the fire devouring her, she cried out.

"I know," he whispered roughly. He kissed her lips. "I feel the same way."

Did he? Suddenly she had to know that he wanted her as much as she wanted him. She ran her palms down his lightly furred chest, gratified as his muscles quivered beneath her fingers.

"Yes." He kissed her again. "Touch me. Feel what you do to me."

And she did. She lowered one hand until she wrapped her fingers tight around his velvet hardness.

"Samantha." He groaned and thrust himself into her hand once, twice, then pulled her hand away. "No more. I can't take any more."

She thrust her hips against his. "Neither can I."

When he turned and leaned over the edge of the bed toward the floor, Sammi reached for the drawer in the nightstand. They both turned back at once, each holding a small foil packet.

Nick was the first to grin. With a devastating flash of lethal dimples, he nodded toward the condom in her hand. "Don't tell me that came with the room."

Sammi blushed. "No, I . . ."

Nick kissed her swiftly, then grinned. "We'll use yours first."

Sammi's heart gave a leap. She couldn't help but smile back at him. "First?"

"First."

He dropped his packet to the floor and reached for hers. With his gaze locked on hers, he tore it open and handed it to her. "You do it."

With shaking fingers, Sammi started rolling the condom into place.

"Samantha?"

Halfway finished, she stopped and looked up at him.

His head was bent back, his eyes squeezed shut. "You better hurry."

Her hands shook harder. Beneath her trembling fingers, Nick grew harder, larger. By the time she finished, his jaws were clenched shut as tightly as his eyes.

Urgency like he'd never felt before tore through Nick. Her touch did things to him no other woman's had. When she drew her hands away he positioned himself between her thighs. He wanted to go slowly, give them both time to savor every sensation. And he would have, too. But then he looked at her.

Her lips were red and swollen from his kisses. Her gaze shot fire clear into his soul. Her lids were lowered; her tongue grazed her lips, and her breath came as fast as his. She was ready—as ready as he was.

No more waiting, no more wanting and not having. Tonight, right now, he would claim her and she would be his.

And he did. And she was.

Slowly, one hot, slick inch at a time, he buried his hard, aching flesh in her softness. She sighed and welcomed him with a flex of her hips, and he was lost, his control gone.

A wild primal rhythm pounded in his head, his blood, his loins. He moved to its beat, slowly at first, then faster and faster as the heat and pressure and agonizing pleasure built.

Sammi met him move for move, thrust for thrust, tearing to shreds any remaining thought he might have had of holding back. Together they soared and gasped. Release came first for Sammi. Nick felt it all around him, heard it in her voice as she cried out his name. He followed her swiftly into the fiery explosion where space and time ceased, where the entire universe consisted of one man, one woman. His woman.

His strength gone, his arms quivering, Nick collapsed half on top of and half off Sammi and rested his head right where it belonged — against her heart. *Mine. She's mine now.*

Sammi woke the next morning to sunlight streaming through the gap in the drapes, and Nick holding her close. She squeezed her eyes shut and prayed for instant sleep. She did not want to wake up and face reality after last night.

But last night hadn't been a dream, it had been real. She and Nick had made love, more than once. When he had touched her with that mixture of tenderness and fierce hunger, she had known then and there that she was hopelessly, irrevocably in love with him. And that way, she knew from past experience, lay disaster.

A cold trembling seized her. Lord, what if he found out she loved him? What if he saw it in her eyes? She wouldn't be able to bear his reaction. He cared for her, she knew, and he had wanted her. But love . . . no, he didn't love her. Would he pity her if he knew how she felt, or would he run as far and fast from her as he could? Either way, she would not be able to handle it.

His arms flexed around her. He was waking up. Panic stiffened her muscles.

He nuzzled the back of her neck and sent shivers down her spine.

Sammi searched the room frantically, looking for something, anything to put an end to their intimacy before she made a complete fool of herself. She spied the bedside clock. Her gasp was genuine. "Nick, wake up! We're going to miss our flight!" She made a lunge for the side of the bed.

"Big deal." Nick clamped his arms around her and pulled her back against his chest. "It's not like we'll get fired, you know. I have an in with your boss. You have an in with your boss."

Sammi froze. Her *boss*. She had just spent the night making wild, incredible love with her *boss*. Lord, what must he think of her?

He turned her in his arms until she faced him. "Come here," he whispered.

Then he kissed her, the most thorough good-morning kiss she had ever experienced. It was a prelude to that all-consuming fire he had built inside her more than once last night. She couldn't . . . she couldn't let . . .

She pulled away and forced a smile without meeting his eyes. "Good morning. Let's don't miss that flight." Before he could stop her, before she allowed herself to give in to his kiss, she slipped from the bed and raced to the bathroom.

Nick watched Sammi's bare backside disappear behind the bathroom door. He felt a sinking sensation in the pit of his stomach. Her eagerness to leave his arms stung.

Maybe, he told himself with a ray of hope, she was merely suffering morning-after shyness. Maybe if he gave her a little time to herself, time she apparently needed, she would feel more at ease with him.

While she showered, Nick went to his room across the hall and did the same, all the while hoping . . . hoping when he saw her next, she would be the same Samantha he had held in his arms last night, the warm, giving woman who couldn't seem to get enough of his touch, whose touch he could not get enough of.

But when he finished packing and knocked on her door, it wasn't Samantha who greeted him, but the ice maiden. She was cool and collected and . . . remote. As distant as a stranger.

233

"Sammi?"

"Oh, good, you're packed. So am I, so let's go."

A dull ache rose from his stomach to his chest and turned into a sharp pain. She was shutting him out, acting as though last night had never happened.

What did you expect? That she would find you so irresistible she would fall at your feet and declare her undying love?

When the elevator arrived, Nick took part of his frustration out on the button for the lobby. Who needed a woman who blew hot one minute, cold the next, damn it.

Still, he wished for just two minutes of privacy with her, just to see if he could break through her shield of indifference. But the two minutes weren't to be. There were other people in the elevator, the lobby was crowded, the cab driver was not only talkative, but had big ears. And once on the plane and in the air, he would have had to raise his voice for her to hear him.

If the 2000 hadn't been in for a scheduled overhaul, they wouldn't have had to make this round trip by commercial air. They would have had privacy. He could have talked to her, and she couldn't have run away.

He clenched his jaws and his fists and wondered how in the hell she could sit calmly next to him reading a damn magazine.

At Dallas-Fort Worth Nick and Sammi had to change planes. On their way to the shuttle that would take them to the other terminal for the last leg of their flight, Nick took her by the arm and pulled her to a semi-private corner.

"Sammi, I want to talk to you about la—"

"I've been meaning to talk to you, too. What do you think? Have you made a decision yet about building a low-cost business jet?"

Nick felt like a huge fist had reached into his chest and ripped out his heart. He had just spent the most incredible night of his life, he had fallen in love—the thought didn't even startle him—and as far as he was concerned, his entire future was at stake. And she wanted to talk about planes?

Something snapped inside him, letting loose a torrent of almost unbearable pain. He tightened his grip on her arm. "Is that what last night was all about—so I would agree to your plans?"

Before the words were out he knew he was making the biggest mistake of his life. He grew even more certain as he watched Sammi's eyes flutter shut, watched the blood drain from her face.

"Sammi, I didn't mean—"

"Let go of me."

Her thin whisper tore into his gut far more sharply than if she had screamed. "Sammi . . ."

"Please. Let go."

He held on. If he let go of her now, he knew he would never get the chance to hold her again. "Samantha, I'm sorry. I didn't mean that. You know I didn't."

"Didn't you?" She opened her eyes and looked at him. "It doesn't matter."

At the dull, lifeless look in her eyes, Nick felt a cold numbness settle over him. His hand slipped from her arm.

He had lost her.

Thirteen

Nick spent the most miserable week and a half of his life trying not to notice how deliberately Sammi avoided him. The only experience in the past that had come close to making him ache so much was when he was seventeen and his mother, bless her, had blurted out in a fit of anger that Henry was not his father.

Nick had thought at the time that nothing could hurt as much as having his mother betray him, having his own father—or the man who had always been that—turn his back on him. Nothing could hurt that much.

He'd been wrong. Seeing the smile on Sammi's face disappear when she spotted him in the hall hurt like hell. Watching her turn and walk away when he came near tore a hole in his chest. Hearing her laughter die . . .

Samantha, I love you.

God, how could he have been such a fool as to hurt her? He had known as those cruel words were coming from his mouth that they weren't true. Sammi would never use him or prostitute herself. She wasn't emotionally capable of such cold calculation.

And even if he didn't believe so strongly in her integrity, he had no choice but to believe her response to him that last night in New Orleans. When he touched her she burned. She had wanted him, genuinely wanted him, the way he wanted her—clear down to her soul. The truth had been there in her eyes, her sighs, the graceful movements of her body.

God, if he didn't stop thinking about her he would go insane. But the truth was, he couldn't, didn't want to.

Over and over he relived every moment of that night. The thrill that shot through him at her trembling touch. The feel of her silken skin beneath his fingers, the taste of her on his lips and tongue. Those dark amber curls that hid the secrets of her womanhood, secrets she willingly, eagerly shared with him. The fresh scent of her hair, the sound of her sighs, those little whimpers she made in the back of her throat. What man wouldn't kill for a woman like her?

Samantha, I want you.

By Friday of their second week back from New Orleans, Nick knew he had to do something. He couldn't take it anymore. Even if she still hated him afterward, he had to apologize for what he had said. He had to try to get through to her, make her see how much he loved her, wanted her, needed her. He couldn't tell her those things—after his crack at the airport, she would never believe him—but maybe he could show her, in time.

The first step was a long-overdue apology.

Friday evening he waited until Sammi left work. He gave her a thirty-minute head start, then followed to her apartment. He pounded on her door until his knuckles throbbed. She didn't answer. Back in the parking lot, he searched for her car. He wouldn't be surprised if she was home and just didn't want to open her door to him. But no, he couldn't find her car.

Damn it! He got back into his car and slammed the door.

He didn't even want to think about where a beautiful woman might be on a Friday night, what she might be doing, whom she might be with. The mere idea tortured Nick with visions of Sammi in another man's arms, kissing his lips, beside him in bed.

Nick squeezed his eyes shut, but the pictures refused to leave. *Sammi! Where are you?*

When he started the car, he wasn't surprised to find his hands trembling.

Unable to face another long, lonely evening at home, Nick drove the streets of Oklahoma

City for more than two hours, not knowing, not caring where he went. It was nearly nine-thirty before he realized the futility of his wanderings. At home or in his car, the night was just as long, just as lonely, the memories of Sammi just as tormenting.

He slowed the car to get his bearings. It only took him a second to realize where he was—at Henry's. Had some long-buried instinct sent him there? Some forgotten childhood habit that sent him crawling for succor and ease to the father who used to solve all his childish problems?

Nick gave a harsh laugh. This was no childish problem that could be smoothed away by a paternal caress, and Henry was not his father.

Still, the urge to go inside was strong enough to get Nick out of his car. He was halfway up the sidewalk before he spotted the back bumper of another car poking out from the rear of the house where the driveway wrapped around. An old car. A beat-up, rusted car. Sammi's car.

Relief flooded him. She wasn't out on a date.

Sweat beaded his palms. She was here. Would she let him talk to her? Could he speak to her in front of Henry?

Henry be damned. Nick had to talk to her.

In two long strides he was at the door. It wasn't locked, so he let himself in. Laughter floated from the den. Sammi's. Something twisted in Nick's chest. Would she ever laugh with him again?

Each step that took him closer to the door down the hall sent his heart pounding harder, faster.

He paused in the open doorway to the den.

"Nick," Henry called. "I didn't hear you. Come in, come in."

But Nick's gaze was locked on Sammi. She sat on the sofa with her back to the door. When Henry called Nick's name, her shoulders stiffened.

"You're just in time," Henry said. "We were looking at old family photos."

Sammi fumbled with something on her lap. A photo album. With jerky movements, she shoved it onto the coffee table before her and rose. "You two probably have a lot to talk about. I didn't realize how late it was. I have to go."

Without a backward glance or another word, she grabbed her purse and sprinted for the door across the room, the one leading to the kitchen. The sound of the back door slamming sent a shaft of pain knifing through Nick's stomach.

Henry rose from his chair, where he'd been sitting facing Sammi. "What the hell," he demanded in a cold voice, "was that all about?

241

What have you done to her?"

Nick gave a bitter bark of laughter. "Just up-holding an old family tradition."

"What's that supposed to mean?"

"Don't worry about it. It's certainly no re-flection on you. I said it was a *family* tradi-tion."

Henry paled.

For the second time in less than two weeks, Nick wished someone had ripped his tongue out before he had opened his mouth. "I'm sorry. I—I seem to be doing that a lot lately—saying things I don't mean."

Henry gave him an odd look, then turned to-ward the bar in the corner. "How about a drink? You'll pardon me for saying so, but you look like you could use one. In fact," he said, glancing over his shoulder at Nick, "you look like hell."

Nick let the comment slide. He hadn't looked in a mirror lately, but he knew, with the minus-cule amount of sleep he'd been getting, he probably did look like hell. It was typical of Henry to say so.

A moment later he took the drink Henry handed him, then started wearing a path from the sofa to the patio door and back.

"You're acting like a caged jungle cat," Henry said. "Sit down and tell me about this family tradition you've been upholding. I as-

242

sume that means you've . . . said something that would have been better left unsaid."

Stunned at Henry's suddenly soft tone, Nick whirled around to face him.

Henry smiled sadly. "The look on your face. Do you honestly believe I never think of what was said between us—the three of us, your mother included—all those years ago? That I never regretted every word?"

Nick felt like the floor had just fallen out from under him. He turned his back on Henry and gulped his drink. He suddenly felt like a child again, a little boy who didn't understand why his daddy had just spanked him. A young man who didn't understand why his whole world had just been destroyed.

He blinked at the stinging behind his eyes. Damn. He cleared his throat. "Look, I didn't come here to dredge up ancient history."

"Why did you come?"

Good question. Nick wished he had an answer. "Are you still seeing Ernestine Winfield?"

Henry made a sound of . . . what, frustration? "Now and then," he said, "but it's nothing to get excited about. We're just friends."

When Nick failed to fill the silence, Henry asked again, "Why did you come?"

"I . . . I'm not sure." Nick started pacing again.

"There are some ties, Nick, that can never be

broken."

Nick knocked back the last of his scotch and water. "What's that supposed to mean?"

In the reflection on the patio door, Nick saw Henry rise and return to the bar. "The two of us are more alike than we realize," Henry said. "You're at least as stubborn as I am."

Nick strode to the bar for a refill. "Meaning?"

"Huh. Look at you. You've got your back up, too stubborn to admit something is wrong. I'll tell you this, Nick—that heart attack I had really opened my eyes. It made me realize how short time can be. I can admit a lot of things now that I never would have before, things you don't want to hear. What you can't admit is that you and Sammi have a problem."

Nick watched Henry plunk ice cubes into both of their glasses and wondered again if Henry should be drinking.

"I remember when you were a kid—"

"More ancient history."

"You used to bring your problems to me," Henry said, ignoring Nick's interruption. Henry gave another sad smile. "Not all your problems. You were pretty good, even as a kid, at solving things. But when you ran up against something you really couldn't deal with, you always brought it to me. You used to tell me I could fix anything."

"Yeah, right." Nick splashed scotch over his ice cubes, foregoing the water he normally added.

"The way I figure it — " Henry added water to his own glass of bourbon. "For the first time in years, you've run up against something you can't handle and you reverted to form — you came to me."

Henry's words were a little too close to Nick's earlier thoughts for comfort.

"Oh, I'm not saying you did it consciously, and I certainly don't expect you to admit it. But let's pretend I'm right. Let's imagine you've finally got a problem — say, with . . . oh, I don't know, say something's wrong between you and Sammi. The two of you can't solve it, so you've come to me for . . . help. The first thing you have to do is tell me what's wrong."

Nick shook his head and started to turn away. "Let it drop, Henry."

Henry grabbed Nick's shoulder and spun him back around, nearly spilling both of their drinks. Henry set his down. "No," he cried. "I won't. I've let too many things drop over the years, things I regret, things . . . No."

That stinging in Nick's eyes was back again. He blinked, but it wouldn't go away.

Henry gripped Nick's arms, his expression urgent, his eyes fierce with pain and sorrow.

245

"The two of us—we've spent so many years hurting each other, maybe it's too late for us. But it's not too late for you and Sammi. Damn it, Nick, whatever it is, fix it, make it right. Don't let it fester into years of bitterness like we did. Don't throw out words like I did, hurtful words you don't mean. Take them back before it's too late."

Nick shrugged off Henry's hold. The lump in his throat wouldn't let him swallow, but he managed to talk around it. "What makes you think I said things I didn't mean?"

Henry's shoulders slumped, and he gave a bitter smile. "Because that's what we do in this family. We get our feelings hurt, then retaliate by saying things we don't mean, things calculated to hurt. I learned the nasty habit from your mother. You learned it from me."

The scotch in Nick's hand started to slosh. He set the drink down and clenched his fists against the pain roiling inside him. "What did you ever say that you didn't mean?"

"That I . . ." Henry took a deep breath, closed his eyes a moment, then met Nick's gaze head on. "That I never wanted to hear you call me Dad again."

A giant fist of pain squeezed Nick's heart. The room spun. He grabbed the edge of the bar for support. He hadn't expected Henry to answer at all, much less with those words. In all the years of their estrangement, through all their bitter arguments and harsh words and occasional semitruces, neither of them had ever, *ever* spoken directly of that night. Somehow speaking of it would have violated the unwritten rules of their animosity.

Now Nick understood why they had avoided it. To think about the night his world had collapsed was one thing. To remember it word for word, tear for tear . . . But to hear the words repeated aloud was unbearable. He squeezed his eyes shut and turned away from the pain. His voice, when it came, felt raw in his throat, sounded harsh to his ear. "You meant every word, and you know it."

"I didn't," Henry cried. "I knew when I said those words I didn't mean them. A thousand times since then I've wanted to call them back, but . . ."

"But what?"

"My pride wouldn't let me. It seemed easier to go on torturing both of us than to admit I was wrong."

"Wrong? What were you wrong about? What was I to you but some stranger's bastard?"

"What were you?" Henry cried. "You were the best part of me, the son I raised for seventeen years. You were everything that was bright and good and perfect in my life. You were the future. Up until that minute when your mother—damn it, Nick, you were *my son*."

"And then I wasn't."

"Weren't you? Aren't you?"

Nick whipped his head around and gaped at Henry. "What's that supposed to mean?"

Henry grasped Nick's upper arms. "It means, what difference does it make whose seed you sprang from? You were my son for seventeen years. If I didn't actually sire you—"

"If?"

"Yes, *if,* damn it." Henry's grip tightened. "Think about it, Nick. What if it wasn't true? What if your mother lied?"

Nick shrugged loose and turned his back. "She didn't and you know it."

"I don't know that. I never have. She could have lied, and if she did, then she's had the last laugh on us all this time."

Nick turned and shook his head. "Why would she have done a thing like that?"

Henry sighed. "Do you remember anything else that was said that night?"

"Not really. Just that she was mad about something. Then again, she was nearly always mad about something."

"Did you ever know why?"

"No. Does it matter at this point?"

"I don't know," Henry said. "Maybe. Did you know she was carrying you when we got married?"

248

Nick rolled his eyes. "God, not another deep, dark family secret. One was more than enough, thank you."

Henry waived Nick's words aside. "I didn't marry her because she was pregnant. I married her because I wanted to. I was crazy about her, you know." Henry smiled softly, sadly. "She was so beautiful."

Nick watched an ice cube role over in his drink. "I remember."

"Anyway," Henry said, "by the time you were two or three, she realized marriage and mother-hood weren't exactly what she thought they would be. The company was still new and there was never any money. I was gone all the time."

With a philosophical shrug, Henry went on. "She got bored, restless, and eventually fed up. Said she wanted a divorce. I told her if she felt she had to go, I wouldn't stop her, but I wouldn't let her take you. I don't think she ever forgave me for that. That's when she started hating me, I think. Anyway, she stayed. Because she loved you."

Nick snorted.

Henry splashed more bourbon into his glass. "I didn't help the situation much, either. I was more married to the company than I was to her. But you, you were my buddy, my best pal, my sidekick. You went everywhere with me. God, I was so thoughtless." He ran his hand through his graying hair.

Nick listened intently as Henry went on to remind him of how close father and son had been. Henry pointed out things Nick had never noticed, or if he had, he had carefully ignored. Over the years, as Henry and Nick had grown closer, when Nick started growing more interested in planes than food, Nick's mother had, justifiably, according to Henry, grown more jealous of the two of them each day.

"When I told her I was teaching you to fly, it was more than she could take. That's when she said she was leaving, that I could have you all to myself if I wanted. Then she dropped her little bombshell."

Nick was grateful Henry didn't repeat the rest of the words spoken that night.

"So she could have lied. She was angry enough, hurt enough, she could have lied just to hurt us. We, you and I, have been willing to believe that she kept her secret for seventeen years, then suddenly told the truth. Why couldn't it really have been the other way around? That the seventeen years were true, and that one final night was a lie? If she hadn't gone and fallen off that damn mountain trying to impress that ski instructor, maybe we could ask her."

Nick remembered too well the stab of pain at the news of his mother's death during his senior year at Oklahoma University. The pain, the guilt, the fresh sense of betrayal.

He shook the memories away. "And if she didn't lie?" *Listen to you, you fool*. He wasn't even arguing with Henry's illogical fantasy! Did he want his father back so badly he would grasp at such a thin straw?

"If she didn't—" Henry pulled Nick around until the two faced each other. "—what difference does it make? You're still the only son I've ever had, the only son I'll ever know. Why did we let her tear us apart? How long are we going to go on denying what we both want?"

The stinging behind Nick's eyes grew worse. His heart thundered. His vision blurred. Wary, he asked, "What is it you think we both want?"

Henry's grip tightened yet again. "I want . . . I want my son back, Nicky."

God! Henry hadn't called him Nicky since Nick was twelve and had manfully proclaimed the name too childish.

"And you, I think, I hope, want your father."

Nick blinked at the moisture in his eyes. He was afraid to believe what he was hearing, yet was unable to deny the yearning in his own heart. He did want his father back. Then he saw the streams of tears on Henry's cheeks.

251

Twenty years of pain and heartache could not stand up to the pleading in Henry's eyes nor the urging of Nick's heart.

With one tentative step, Nick was back in his father's arms. The two men held each other in an embrace fierce enough to burn away all the bad things that had passed between them through the years, leaving, at the end of their emotionally cleansing storm, the promise of a whole new future.

It was a long while before either was willing to let go. Nick stepped back first, more than slightly embarrassed at the wetness on his cheeks. He ducked his head and swiped at it.

Henry laughed. With a shaking hand, he pushed Nick's hands away and wiped his son's cheeks. "Snot-nosed kid."

Nick felt a sheepish grin, then took a swipe at Henry's cheeks. "Yeah, but look who's talking, old man."

Henry stilled. His wobbly smile died. "Whatever is true, whatever isn't, know this, Nick. You're my son, and I love you."

Nick pulled his father to him again and wrapped his arms around the man who had raised him. In a choked voice, he said, "I love you, too, Dad."

It was several long moments before Nick felt steady enough to pull away.

Henry let him go with a brusque, "Well!

Let's freshen up these drinks."

A moment later, fresh drinks in hand, the two sat side by side on the sofa.

"You want to tell me what happened between you and Sammi?"

Holding his drink steady on the arm of the sofa, Nick slouched and dropped his head to the padded back. "What else? I opened my mouth. I got my ego bruised. I thought . . . I thought we were getting close. Then out of the blue she pulled her ice maiden routine."

"And it hurt?"

Nick shrugged one shoulder. "Yeah. It hurt."

"So you said something you didn't mean. So what are you going to do about it?"

"I've been trying like hell to apologize, but as you saw tonight, she won't let me within ten feet of her."

"So you're going to give up?"

Give up? On Sammi? He couldn't. God help him, not that. He sat up. "Of course not."

Henry slapped him on the back. "Atta boy."

"But I don't know how much longer I can stand her cold shoulder."

Henry crossed his legs and tugged at the knee of his slacks. "Remember the time when you were nine and the other boys said they weren't going to let an egghead with straight A's play on their baseball team?"

Nick frowned, then chuckled at the memory.

"I remember," Henry said. "You just ignored them, stepped up to the plate with your bat, and took the best pitch that little Watson brat had to offer. Knocked it clear over the fence."

"This is a little different, Dad."

They both smiled at how easily the word *Dad* slid off Nick's tongue.

"True," Henry admitted. "But what about the Maverick?"

Nick rubbed at the tension in the back of his neck. The Maverick. How many painful subjects could a man deal with in one night? "More ancient history."

"If you say so. I'm just remembering when you first came up with the idea and I called it foolish. I put every roadblock I could find in your path. But you didn't let anything stop you. You designed it, you test-flew it, you were *that close*." Henry held his thumb and forefinger a half-inch apart. "That close."

"And then I lost it all. The Maverick's gone, and you know it."

Henry gave him an odd look. "If you say so."

"What does any of this have to do with Sammi?"

"You're in love with her, aren't you?"

"That's beside the point."

"It's exactly the point. If you're in love with her, if you want her bad enough, you'll put at

254

least as much effort into solving your problem with her as you did with baseball and the Maverick."

"I lost interest in baseball, and I had the Maverick yanked out from under me."

"So maybe in twenty years you'll lose interest in Sammi. Maybe some other man will come along and steal her out from under your nose. Maybe we'll all fall off the face of the earth a week from next Tuesday. And if we don't, maybe we should both just sit on this damn couch and wait to die of old age."

Nick grinned all the way home. Henry—his *father*—had finally let the subject of Sammi drop, but the two men had gone on to talk for hours. They had relived a few moments of the past, good memories, and talked about making new ones.

Never in his wildest fantasies had Nick dared during the past twenty years to dream of feeling like a son again. A dream so futile would have hurt too much.

But now a miracle had happened. He had his father back again. The stinging behind his eyes and the lump in his throat returned just remembering that first tentative step they had taken toward each other a few hours ago, a lifetime ago, it seemed.

Life was damned near perfect. Or would be,

if he had Sammi at his side.

What happened, Sammi? How am I going to get you back?

No answer came, but that didn't deter Nick. He would get her back in his arms, in his life. Somehow. He refused to settle for occasional glimpses of her from down the hall. He wanted more than that from Samantha Carmichael. Much more. He wanted her in his life. He wanted her smiles, her laughter. Her friendship. Her love.

He wanted . . . he wanted Sammi's heart.

Fourteen

Saturday morning Sammi scowled at her reflection in her bathroom mirror. The circles beneath her eyes were even darker this morning. And no wonder. Running into Nick every time she turned around at work was bad enough. But running into him at Henry's had been more than she could handle. She had let down her guard because she thought at Henry's she would be safe from Nick's presence.

She'd been wrong. And she had paid for it with another sleepless night, as well she should have. Every time she went to Henry's, it seemed like Nick showed up. She should have known the other night wouldn't be any different.

Something had to give. She knew she couldn't keep avoiding Nick at work. It was childish, it was counterproductive, and she was being much too obvious about it. More than once in the past week whispered conversations had stopped abruptly at her approach.

She had made a mistake. A big one. But she hadn't fallen in love with Nick on purpose, hadn't wanted it to happen at all. Because of her feelings for him, she had made a severe error in judgment that night in New Orleans.

She had paid for it the next day when Nick's words had ripped her to shreds.

The incident was over. Sammi knew she had to either learn to put it in the past and return to some type of normal relationship with Nick, or she had to find another job. She couldn't go on the way she had been.

She knew Nick wanted to talk to her. She supposed, if she intended to stay at Elliott Air, she was going to have to let him. But God, the mere thought of facing him, of standing close enough to see his eyes and remember the accusation she had seen in them—she didn't know if she had the strength.

Maybe she shouldn't even try. Maybe it would be best for everyone if she simply left the company.

You mean easiest for you, don't you?

Sammi frowned. Was that Jim's voice? She hadn't heard it inside her head in weeks.

Yeah, that's right. Blame Jim.

Oh. It was her voice. A peculiar feeling came over her. She cocked her head, and from somewhere inside, the voice came again.

You blamed Jim for what went wrong with your marriage. Now you can blame Nick if you quit your job. It's always someone else's fault, isn't it?

Sammi sat on the edge of the tub and covered her face with both hands. The truth battered her from all sides. She had tried so hard to please Jim that she had turned herself into a doormat. If she had stood up to him, perhaps he would have respected her more. If she had held some outside interest, other than simply trying to be the perfect little homemaker, maybe he would have found her more interesting.

But no, instead of thinking for herself, instead of taking charge of her own life, she had done what she thought Jim wanted, what he said he wanted. She had taken the easy way.

Now, here she was again, running from confrontation, taking the easy way out. If Nick really thought so little of her as to accuse her of bartering with her body . . .

The mere thought of his accusation that day in DFW still had the power to knock the breath from her lungs.

Another woman might have slapped his face for such an outrageous, insulting comment. But Sammi had turned in on herself and held on to the pain.

Well, no more.

She rose from the edge of the tub and turned on the shower. Finding a new job was not best for her. She liked the one she had. She would just have to tell Nick to leave her alone. If he didn't like it, he could fire her.

But could she do it, and learn to behave normally around him when her heart cracked at the mere thought of him?

She would have to. He had called a staff meeting for Monday. She would have to face him then.

She thanked God that *this* memo hadn't disappeared. She shuddered to think what connotation Nick would put on her missing the meeting. With the way she had been acting lately, he would think she was hiding from him, and be justified in thinking so. Thank God that memo had been on her desk.

In fact, as far as she knew, none of her memos had disappeared lately. She just wished she could say the same for her files. She had spent the past two days searching her office for the information she had collected in New Orleans on the SJ30 and the CitationJet. She distinctly remembered leaving both files on the center of her desk Wednesday evening. Thursday morning, they had been gone.

Was someone playing games with her, or was she more distracted than she realized?

She didn't know, but she intended to find out.

Meanwhile, she was going to do something about her wardrobe. She didn't much like being accused of wearing camouflage.

Monday morning Nick steeled himself for the first day of his campaign to get Sammi back.

He unlocked his office door and nearly fell when his foot slipped on a folded piece of paper on the floor. Someone must have slid it under his door early this morning or over the weekend—sometime after he left Friday evening.

He picked the paper up and carried it to his desk. There he flipped it open, then froze. Unevenly printed block letters, the type a child might manage, practically leapt off the page.

CARMICHAEL WILL RUIN
THE COMPANY—
SHE'S MAKING A FOOL OF YOU!
GET RID OF HER.

The heat of rage flushed through him hot and swift. If he ever got his hands on the culprit who wrote the note, Nick wouldn't be responsible for his own actions.

The note obviously came from an employee, but who? Who would write such a thing? Who despised Sammi that much?

"Nick?"

He jerked his head up. He hadn't heard Marie come to his door. "Yes?"

"You asked me to remind you—staff meeting in fifteen minutes."

"Right." Carefully he folded the paper and tucked it into his pocket. "Thanks."

When Marie left the doorway Nick closed his eyes and took a deep breath. He had to put the note out of his mind. Later he would find the one responsible, and when Nick was finished with him, the sorry bastard would regret ever having learned to write.

But first he had a meeting. An important one. Aside from business, he had a plan to put into action, to make Sammi talk to him.

When Sammi walked into the conference room the staff meeting was already in progress. She looked at J. W., at Vic, at anyone other than Nick. Yet her gaze was drawn to him involuntarily. He looked . . . relieved?

"Anything wrong?" he asked.

"No. I wasn't notified you intended to start early."

"We started on time, at eight forty-five," Nick said easily.

Sammi frowned. "My memo said nine o'clock."

J. W. laughed. "Mine said eight forty-five."

"Yeah," Bob Loflin, the controller said. "Mine, too."

"Maybe you need glasses, Sammi," Vic offered with a smirk.

Sammi clenched her jaw.

"Now, gentlemen." Nick grinned. "If you want to survive around this lady, I'll give you some advice. Never pick on her when she's wearing new clothes. You just never know what to expect."

Sammi's mouth dropped open as her cheeks heated. What in the world—

"Have a seat, Sammi." Nick stood and held out a chair for her.

It was a full moment before Sammi could move. She couldn't imagine what had gotten into him. His remark had to have been a reference to her turquoise dress. What the hell was going on?

For Sammi, the entire meeting passed in a buzz. If her life depended on it, the only thing she could have said about the next thirty minutes of her life was that Nick kept smiling at her.

What had happened to the contrite man with the hang-dog look who had been trying to corner her for nearly two weeks just so he could apologize?

Sammi blinked. One by one the others were leaving the room. Nick stood near the door talking to Jerry Hanson from Quality Control. If she could get her legs to work, she would slip past them without being noticed and get to her office. Maybe there she could think straight and figure out what Nick was up to.

Just as she passed through the doorway, thinking she had made good her escape, Nick called her name. She stopped and turned slowly back to him.

"I like the new suit." His voice held an intimate tone, yet was clear enough and loud enough for Marie to hear at her desk out in the hall. Sammi knew, because Marie was gaping at the two of them. Then he did the most incredible thing. He winked at Sammi. In plain sight of everyone. "You look great in it," he said. "I'll . . . see you later?"

Sammi stared at him a moment in shock, then whirled around and fled down the hall to her office. There, she slammed the door and threw herself down on her chair.

What did he think he was doing? What the *hell* did he think he was doing, damn him? He was deliberately leading the staff to think there was something going on between them. Oh, she had seen that sparkle in his eyes, all right. He was being very deliberate.

What she couldn't understand was why?

By the next morning, when she drove to work in a downpour that thankfully stopped before she parked her car, she still had no idea what had possessed Nick to act the way he had yesterday. All morning she tried to work, with no success. She couldn't get her mind off Nick's bizarre behavior at the staff meeting.

She threw her pencil down in frustration. Maybe a walk over to the paint building to check the latest data on the Video Jet would clear her mind. She grabbed her safety glasses on the way out of her office, but didn't remember to put them on until Gus hollered at her when she passed Quality Control.

"You're supposed to wear them, not carry them!" he shouted.

"Right! Sorry!" Feeling like an idiot for forgetting, she slipped the glasses on.

At the hangar door, Sammi stopped and stared with dismay at the giant puddle—it was ten feet across if it was an inch—standing between her and the paint building. Either she could ruin her brand new shoes, which she refused to do, or walk all the way around and use the east door.

She turned around to head that way and ran smack into a broad, hard chest. Nick's chest.

"Hi there," he said with a dimple-flashing grin. "It's good to see you, too."

Sammi cast him a glare and stepped aside. "Excuse me."

She meant to walk around him, but he stopped her with a hand on her arm. "Going over to the paint hangar?"

She didn't want to answer him, to talk to him, or even to think about him, let alone be near him.

"Come on," he said, tugging her toward the door. "I was headed that way myself."

"Nick, I—"

The rest of her words ended in a shriek as Nick swung her up into his arms and started across the wide puddle.

"What the devil do you think you're doing?" she whispered angrily in his ear.

With his gaze trained straight ahead and a Cheshire-cat grin firmly in place, he said, "Playing the gentleman. Do you mind?"

"Yes, I mind!" *I mind the tingling racing through my body just because you're touching me. I mind the urge I feel to put my arms around your neck. I mind!*

In the doorway to the paint hangar Nick set her back on her feet. "There you go, safe and sound. Don't thank me, I was glad to do it."

Sammi opened her mouth, then snapped it shut. At least a dozen people had stopped work and were watching her and Nick. She had never felt more like screaming in her life.

Nick winked at her again, then tucked his hands into his pants pockets and walked off toward the last hangar, whistling " 'Oh What A Beautiful Morning'."

Sammi ground her teeth in frustration. Nick had obviously come up with another game to play, and it seemed she was "it." She just wished she knew what the rules and object were.

She started toward the Video Jet machine in the back of the building, but didn't make it ten feet before someone called her name from behind. Gus had followed her.

He took her arm and pulled her to a relatively quiet spot along the west wall. "Are you out of your mind, girl, letting him carry on like that? Or don't you care what everybody thinks?"

"Of course I care!" she cried. "Trust me, Gus.

Nobody is more stunned that I am by Nick's actions."

"You just watch yourself, Sammi. The talk around here is fast and vicious. Everybody knows your ninety-day probation is about up. Next thing they're going to start wondering is—"

"Stop it! Don't you dare say another word. You know me better than that, Gus."

"Do I? I thought I did. After two out-of-town trips in a month with just the two of you, then the way you've both been acting since you got back from New Orleans—I don't know, Sammi. I don't think I know you anymore. It's pretty damned obvious what's going on. I just hope you know what you're doing."

"Gus—"

But he didn't let her finish. Her friend and mentor turned his back and walked away, leaving her standing alone against the wall with dozens of eyes piercing her with speculation.

Trembling under the censure directed her way, Sammi forgot the data she had come for and made her way back to her office. For the next two days she barely came out. The one time she did venture down the hall proved disastrous.

She was headed for Marie's desk to return a file she had borrowed, when Darla called out that Sammi's phone was ringing. Still walking forward, Sammi looked over her shoulder toward Darla. "Would you get it and ask them to hold? I'll be right there."

The few steps she had taken without watching where she was going had been a few too many. She ran smack in to someone. The hauntingly familiar feel of that tall, muscled shape told her exactly who that someone was.

Warm hands clasped her arms and steadied her. His deep voice held laughter in its tone. "Well, hello to you, too."

Sammi jumped back. "Sorry. I wasn't watching where I was going."

Nick flashed those lethal dimples. "Don't apologize. It was my pleasure."

From the corner of her eye Sammi saw Marie staring at them with her mouth hanging open. Sammi knew just how the woman felt. She, too, couldn't believe what was happening.

Then Nick caressed her cheek briefly. A hot shudder shot through her at his gentle touch. His smile turned crooked. "I've got an appointment right now, but I'll see you later."

The intimate tone, soft yet loud enough to carry, left her not knowing whether to scream or melt.

Then he was gone, striding down the hall, whistling " 'I Found My Thrill on Blueberry Hill'."

Sammi thought seriously about bashing him in the head, but she doubted the file folder in her hand would do the trick. She gritted her teeth and slammed the folder down on Marie's desk and stomped back to her office. She only came out one other time all day, and that was to go to the ladies' room.

Even the privacy of the restroom stall wasn't safe. While there, she heard the outer door open. She recognized Darla and Marie's voices instantly.

"He can't keep his eyes off her. It's disgusting."

"Oh, I don't know," Marie said. "I wouldn't mind having a man like Nick panting after me."

"Yeah, especially if he was your boss. Talk about job security. I guess we know how her ninety-day probation will turn out."

Sammi yanked the stall door open. In her rage, she didn't pay attention to the force she used. The door slammed against the wall and knocked loose a chip of paint.

Marie and Darla jerked as if shot.

"The first rule of bathroom gossip," Sammi said between clenched teeth, "is to always make sure the stalls are empty before you start in. You might try it sometime, ladies."

As she sailed past them and out the door, Sammi took grim pleasure in their twin guilty, embarrassed blushes.

Thursday morning when she got to work the final straw hit her back. There in the middle of her desk sat a crystal bud vase bearing a single red rose just starting to open its velvet petals. The attached card read, "Yours, Nick."

For one brief moment her eyes stung and she

wished . . . oh, God, she wished it was true. She wished Nick was hers, that he belonged to her, and she to him, that he loved her, that she could admit her love for him.

If wishes were dollars, I'd own the world.

But she didn't want the world. She only wanted . . . the impossible.

What she did not want was one more minute of whatever game Nick was playing. Yours, indeed.

He had made exquisite, passionate love to her, then cut her to the quick with his insulting question at the airport. Since then he had teased her, humiliated her in front of her co-workers, caused her to be the hottest topic on the company grapevine since their previous receptionist had been caught naked in the janitor's closet with one of the production crew last year. Now, flowers.

It was too much. She couldn't, wouldn't take anymore. She spent several minutes working up a good, healthy rage by remembering each ridiculous, asinine stunt Nick had pulled in the past days. Just about the time she was wishing she could get her hands around his throat, she grabbed the bud vase and marched down the hall. Her heels struck the tile floor in a forceful rhythm, echoing her progress down the corridor.

"What a pretty flower," Darla said as Sammi passed her desk without slowing. "Who . . ."

Gus stepped out of J. W.'s office as Sammi

neared. "Good morning."

She merely glared at him and kept going. She marched past Marie's desk without acknowledgment, straight into Nick's office. She slammed the door behind her, stood across the desk from him, and whacked the vase onto the smooth mahogany surface with a solid *thud*. The satisfaction of seeing Nick flinch at the sound was not enough to cool the fire in her veins.

She placed her knuckles on the edge of his desk and leaned toward him. "I'm not leaving this office—and neither are you—until you tell me what the devil you think you're doing."

He leaned back in his chair and closed his eyes. He whispered something that sounded like, "Finally," but she wasn't sure.

"What?"

He opened his eyes and met her gaze steadily. "I was about to run out of outrageous ideas. I'm glad the flower finally did the trick."

Fifteen

Nick watched her eyes widen, then grow wary. "Trick? What trick?"

He shrugged with a casualness he didn't feel. Inside, his heart was pounding. "I wanted to talk to you, but you wouldn't let me get within ten feet. I had to think of a way to make you come to me."

"You what?"

"You heard me."

"You mean you did all this," she waved an arm in the air, "you embarrassed and humiliated me in front of the entire company, made everybody around think we're, we're—"

"Sleeping together?"

A gurgling sound of rage came from her throat. "Yes! That's exactly what they think. But are they talking about you all over the plant? Nooo, sir. I'm the one—" She jabbed a thumb at her chest. "—whose name is being dragged through the mud. I'm the one being accused of sleeping with the boss just to keep my job. Damn you, Nick."

She took her hands from the desk, straightened and ran her fingers through her hair. "I knew that night in New Orleans was a mistake. I just had no idea—"

"No!" Nick was out of his chair and around his desk before she could react. He grabbed her by the shoulders and only barely restrained from shaking her. "That night was not a mistake," he said fiercely.

She winced under his grip.

He jerked his hands away. "I'm sorry. I didn't mean to hurt you. But damn it, Sammi, how can you call what happened between us a mistake?"

"How can you even ask that, after everything you've done since then, starting the very next day at the airport."

"Your memory is selective. Let's start a little earlier in the day, shall we?"

She blinked in surprise. "What are you talking about?"

"I'm talking about two people who had just spent the most incredible night in their lives— and don't try to deny it, because I know better, I know you felt what I did. Then I woke up the next morning and not only wouldn't you kiss me, you wouldn't even look me in the eye. All

273

you could think about was getting back to work."

He could tell by the flush on her cheeks she remembered every detail of that morning, and the night before.

"Hell, I even tried to talk to you about it, to ask you what was wrong. All you wanted to talk about was making planes. *That's* why I opened my mouth and said something I didn't mean. I knew you wouldn't use me the way I was accusing you, that you wouldn't lower yourself like that. I knew it, Sammi. That's what I've been trying to tell you all this time. That I'm sorry for what I said, that I never meant it."

"Wait a minute." Sammi took a step back and doubled up her fists. He had obviously not made much of a dent in that hard head of hers. "Are you saying you have spent the past week deliberately trying to make me mad enough to come to your office so you could apologize for making me mad two weeks ago?"

Her voice had risen in volume with each word, until by the time she finished she was practically screeching at him. But Nick wasn't disappointed. He would take that any day over that damned cold mask she had used in the past.

"I did more than make you mad two weeks ago. I hurt you, and I'm sorry."

"Yes," she whispered. "You hurt me then. You hurt me yesterday, and the day before that, and the day before that, and I still don't understand why."

He started to speak, but she held up her hand.

"I don't want to know. Just stop it. If you think I should quit my job, say so. If not, then leave me alone, Nick. Please."

"Sammi . . ."

But she was past him and out the door before he could stop her.

Damn. He had blown it. He had tried to straighten things out between them and had managed instead to make things worse. He clenched his fists and closed his eyes. What was he supposed to do now? Just let her go? Leave her alone, as she asked?

He couldn't, God help him. Not now, not ever.

He would try again to make her understand, and do it right now.

He left his office and walked straight to hers. He stepped in and closed the door behind him. She stood reading a sheet of paper at her desk. Her face was white as death, and she shook so hard the paper rattled.

"Sammi?"

She jerked and cried out. With a hand to her chest, she said, "You scared the life out

275

of me. I didn't hear you."

"What's wrong?"

"Oh, uh . . ." She waved the paper around, then folded it in half and tossed it onto her desk. "Nothing."

But Nick knew better. A cold lump settled in the pit of his stomach. He had caught only a glimpse as she had waved the paper around, but that was all he needed to tell him she had just received a note similar to the one he himself had received, the one that had warned him to fire Sammi.

He held out his hand. "Let me see the note."

"Note? Oh, you mean this? It's nothing, really."

"Nice try, but your voice is shaking nearly as much as your hands. Now let me see it." He stepped toward the desk.

Sammi blocked his path. "Nick, it's . . . it's personal. Really."

"I can just imagine."

Her eyes widened. "Oh my God, you got one, too."

Instead of answering, he reached around her and grabbed the note. He swore with every word he read:

WHEN HE GETS TIRED OF YOU,
HE'LL FIRE YOU.
QUIT NOW, BITCH.

That he had received a similar missive, obvi-

276

ously written by the same person, was one thing. But Sammi . . . Rage like he had never known before nearly strangled him. How dare someone say such a thing to Sammi!

And it was his own damn fault. When he had decided how to make Sammi come to him, he hadn't fully considered the consequences she might have to pay. Damn it! How could he have been so stupid?

"Who would do such a thing?" Sammi asked in a stricken voice. "Who hates me that much?"

It did seem to Nick that someone had it in for Sammi. Her note was much more vicious than the one he'd received. But he wasn't about to point that out. "Nobody hates you," he told her. "Somebody is just trying to run you off. What I have to figure out is why, and who."

"We," Sammi said. "What *we* have to figure out."

She seemed steadier now, with a little color returning to her cheeks. He longed to brush his lips across those cheeks, tangle his hands in her hair, make her forget the note, her anger with him, everything. Yet he couldn't. First of all, he seriously doubted she would let him. Plus, he had work to do. He had to find out who was at the bottom of this.

"Let's go back to my office and see what we can figure out. We can't do much in this broom closet of yours. How do you stand it in here?"

"I like my office just fine, thank you very much."

That's better, he thought. Now she looked like his Sammi again, rather than a scared, lost child. Still, the constriction in his chest did not ease. She was hurting, and he was responsible.

They went back to his office and closed the door. Sammi sat on one of the chairs before his desk. Nick paced to the window and watched a Cherokee land on the runway.

"When you left here a few minutes ago," he asked, "did you see anyone in the hall? Anyone who could have been in your office?"

She sighed. "Marie was at her desk. I think . . . J. W. was just walking back into his office. Gus was leaving, going back downstairs. And Darla was at her desk. Do you think it could have been one of them?"

Nick rubbed the back of his neck and turned to face her. "I don't like to think it was anyone who works here, but it was someone with easy access to your office. Someone who wouldn't be noticed at my end of the hall, either."

"When . . . when did you get your note?"

It was Nick's turn to sigh. "A few days ago."

"What did it say?"

He wanted to lie to her, but he couldn't. "Just that I should get rid of you because I was making a fool of myself."

She gave him a frown. "You deserved that."

278

"Yeah, tell me about it. Purposely making a fool of myself hasn't been easy."

"One of these days maybe I'll take the time to figure out just why you did it."

"One of these days I'll explain it to you. But first we have to figure out who's writing these notes. Earlier you said everybody thought—"

"I know what I said."

"Has anyone said anything to you about it, about us?"

"Only half the plant."

Nick closed his eyes briefly. "I'm sorry."

"Would you quit saying that?" she demanded.

"Well I am," he responded. "Now, which half of the plant? Who, specifically?"

She sighed again. "Marie and Darla were having a field day gossiping about us in the ladies' room the other day. That day it rained and you . . . carried me. Gus . . ."

"Gus what?"

"Gus wasn't pleased with what he saw happening. But then he hasn't been too happy with me about a lot of things lately."

Nick narrowed his eyes in thought.

"No," Sammi said. "It couldn't be Gus. He might be upset with me now and then, but he's my friend. He wouldn't do this."

Nick's phone rang. Marie informed him Henry was there wanting to see him. "Send him in."

An instant later Henry swept into the room and shut the door behind him with a firm *click*. Before Nick could speak, Henry glanced to Sammi then back to Nick and demanded, "What the hell is going on around here?"

Nick noted with slight amusement that, while he may have his father back, apparently having a son again hadn't mellowed Henry much. "What, precisely, are you talking about?" Nick asked.

"I'm talking about the phone call I got last night. Somebody disguised his voice like some two-bit actor in a B-grade movie. Warned me to force you to get rid of Sammi before she destroyed the company."

Nick felt his hackles rise.

"Now tell me just what the hell is going on," Henry demanded again.

Sammi sat, outwardly calm, inwardly shaking, while the two men discussed the situation, and her, as if she weren't even in the room.

"Let's have a look at Sammi's personnel file. It's got records of all her projects, as well as the people she worked with the past three years. Maybe there's something in there."

"That's a waste of time," Nick said. "I can tell you exactly what's in Sammi's file. Two sheets of paper, one with her name, address, and social security number, the other listing the date she was hired and the dates of her promotions."

"Two sheets? Don't be ridiculous. That file was at least an inch and a half thick the last time I saw it," Henry said.

"I tell you, I pulled it my first day here, on your advice, if you'll recall, and it held two sheets of paper, nothing more."

"Well," Sammi said. "It seems you can quit blaming yourself, Nick."

"What do you mean?"

"I mean, if someone went to the trouble to clean out my file that long ago, this is no spur of the minute campaign to get rid of me. Someone has been planning it for a long time. Which also might explain the memos I don't get and my files that keep disappearing."

"What files?" Nick snapped. "You've never mentioned anything missing to me."

Sammi sighed. She explained about the memos she found in her trash; the last one, not in the trash, but bearing the wrong time for the meeting; the files that disappeared for days, then reappeared right on her desk.

"Why didn't you tell me any of this?"

"And have you think I'm totally incompetent? You told me the day you came here you thought my job was superfluous, and me right along with it."

"Damn it, Sammi—"

"Save it, you two," Henry said. "The most obvious answer to this, since it's Sammi somebody's wanting to get rid of, is that you," Henry said to Nick, "have an overardent secret admirer who's eaten alive with jealousy over your attentions to Sammi."

"Don't be ridiculous, Dad."

Dad? Sammi had never heard Nick use that word in reference to Henry before. Now that she thought about it, the two did seem to be more in tune with each other than she had ever imagined they could be.

"I haven't been anything other than polite and friendly with any woman in the plant."

"Maybe too friendly?" Henry suggested.

Nick's gaze met hers. The sudden heat in his eyes made her weak. "Only with Sammi," he said softly.

"Still," Henry said, " 'a woman scorned,' and all that."

Nick shook his head. "It's possible, I guess, but I don't buy it. Neither note suggested we stay away from each other. Both notes wanted Sammi gone from here completely. And then there's her file. That leads me to believe somebody might be more jealous over her job, her importance in the company, than over whatever they think is going on between the two of us."

Sammi spent the next hour answering Nick's questions as to who she had worked closely with

282

on her various job assignments from the day she was hired. Who might be jealous of her fast rise to the top. Every time Gus's name came up, as it did frequently, Nick and Henry looked at each other.

"Stop it, you two. Gus couldn't have written those notes. He and I have been friends since I came here."

"Sammi," Henry said gently. "Gus has been after a promotion since before you were hired. Isn't it possible he could resent you for shooting past him so quickly? He's worked here for fifteen years, and along comes a young woman with no previous experience, and suddenly she's being promoted over him. You have to admit . . ."

Sammi defended Gus with all her might, but Nick and Henry wouldn't listen. No matter what she said, they were convinced he was the one behind the notes.

"Let's get him up here," Henry suggested.

"No!" Sammi cried.

"Yes," Nick said firmly. "You said yourself he was angry with you the other day. You also said you saw him in the hall just before you found that note this morning." Nick picked up the phone.

When Gus arrived a few minutes later, Sammi found she couldn't face him. She stood at the window with her back to the room.

Outside, the day was clear and sunny, a beautiful November day. So pretty, so pleasant. A far cry from what was taking place behind her in Nick's office.

"Henry," Gus cried. "Glad to see you. What's up?"

Sammi crossed her arms and clenched her fists. *Please don't let it be Gus. Please.* He was her friend. He couldn't be the one who hated her. Please, God, not him.

Nick didn't mince words. "Were you in Sammi's office this morning?"

"This morning? Yeah, I stopped by, but she wasn't there. What's going on?"

"I understand you, ah, weren't too happy with her the other day when I carried her through the water over to the paint hangar."

"Sammi?" Gus said. "What's going on?"

Sammi turned to him. "I . . ."

His face flushed. He straightened his shoulders and eyed everyone in the room. "What I said to Sammi was private, between friends. If I was out of line, I'm sorry. In fact, that's why I was looking for you this morning, Sammi, to apologize for what I said."

"You went to her office to apologize?" Nick asked.

"That's right."

"Did you leave a note?"

"No, I didn't leave a note. Somebody want to

284

tell me what this third degree is all about? If you've got something to ask me, just ask, damn it."

For the first time since Gus entered the room, Sammi looked at Nick. A fist of pain squeezed her chest. This was hurting him. He didn't want to believe Gus guilty. Then she watched his face change as his resolve apparently hardened.

"All right," Nick said, "I'll ask. Did you write these?" He placed the two notes, one of which Sammi hadn't read yet, side by side on his desk.

If Sammi had needed reassurance that Gus was innocent, she had it. She hoped Nick and Henry saw the honest shock on his face as he read the notes.

"Good God! Who—" His head shot up, and he glared at Nick. "You think *I* . . . ? Good God. You *do* think I wrote these!"

Nick's jaw flexed. "Did you?"

"No!"

But the strangled cry wasn't Gus's. It came from the open doorway. Nick, Henry, Gus, and Sammi all whirled to find Darla clutching the door, tears streaming down her pale cheeks.

"It wasn't Gus," she said, sobbing. "It was me. I did it. Oh, Gus, I'm sorry. I was just trying to help. Trying to get rid of her so they would see you were the one who should have been promoted. You should have had her job. I did it for you, Gus. I did it—" She gulped.

"—for you!"

For several long minutes the only sound in the room was Darla's quiet crying.

"Darla," Gus finally said. "I don't understand."

She swiped at her eyes then flung her head up. "What don't you understand," she said fiercely. "That I'm in love with you?"

The stunned expression on Gus's face told everyone, including Darla, that her words were a shock.

"Yes," she cried, "I love you. You're good and kind and smart, and you should have been the one," she said with a touch of venom, "who got promoted. But as long as *she's* around, you'll never stand a chance. As long as she's around, you'll never look at me. Don't you see? I did it for you, for us, Gus."

Then she whirled around and ran from the room, the sounds of her sobs echoing down the hall.

Henry made as if to rise.

"No," Gus said. "I better go after her, talk to her. I . . . didn't know. I had no idea."

He looked so stricken, Sammi's heart ached for him.

"Gus . . . I'm sorry," Nick said.

Gus gave him a long look, then glanced at Sammi and back. The two men shared some secret message she couldn't read.

286

Gus nodded. "I think I understand. I would have done the same thing."

Gus took off after Darla, and Henry sank back down to his chair. "I've never been so glad to be wrong in my entire life."

"Me, too," Nick said with feeling.

"What—" Sammi had to stop and clear her throat. "What happens now?"

"Darla finds a new job," Nick said grimly.

After a moment of heavy silence, Henry finally spoke. "Well, I'm glad that's over with. You two probably have a few things to discuss. I'll be going."

"Henry," Sammi protested.

"Thanks, Dad, you're right. Sammi and I have some things to talk over."

Sammi quailed. Not again. She couldn't deal with Nick one on one again today. But unless she wanted to stomp out of the room like a spoiled child, she didn't see any way out of the present situation. One spoiled-child stomping-off per day was about her limit, and she had already pulled it once this morning.

But that didn't mean she had to let the conversation get personal again. The minute Henry closed the door on his way out, Sammi took a deep breath and turned to Nick. "I do have some things to talk to you about."

Nick motioned her toward the chair before his desk. "All right. Business, or personal?"

Be assertive. Keep control. She sat down and crossed her legs. "Business," she said crisply.

Nick sat down then. "Fine. We'll do business first."

First. Oh, Lord. That meant he wasn't finished with their earlier discussion.

"What did you want to talk about?"

Unfortunately, the only topic she could think of that they hadn't already discussed was one she would rather shy away from. Still, it had to be a less painful subject than whatever Nick wanted to talk about.

She took another deep breath and plunged in. "My ninety-day probation is up tomorrow. What happens then?"

Nick arched an eyebrow. "I was wondering if you remembered." He folded his arms and leaned his elbows on his desk. "What happens is, your probation ends, and you keep doing your job."

She wanted to sag with relief. One hurdle crossed. "Do I work for you, or J. W.?"

He gave her a half-grin. "I imagine by now you wish I would put you under J. W., but no, you work for me, as a full director, equal to all the other directors in Operations. If I hire a Vice President of Operations, you'll work for him."

Sammi held back a sigh. Her job was safe. Her heart wasn't. She had to keep him talking

288

about work until she could make a graceful escape. She would even settle for semigraceful. "What about the Skybird?"

Nick leaned back in his chair and pursed his lips. "When we finish our current contracts, which you know won't be for months yet, and if the Product Liability Bill passes Congress, we'll retool and start production."

Sammi's heart skipped a beat. She leaned forward and gripped the edge of his desk. "On the Skybird 2000?"

"Yes."

"Do you mean it?"

His lips relaxed then, and he grinned. And flashed those damn dimples. "You're sure hard to convince." He came around his desk and sat on the chair next to hers. "Hell yes, I mean it. The Skybird 2000 goes back into production — if the bill passes."

"And you think it will."

"Yes. Sammi . . ."

Oh, God, he was going to get personal. "What about my idea on the low-cost business jet?"

"No."

"No?" She blinked. "Just like that? No?"

"By the time we come up with a design and spend five years getting FAA certification, we will have missed the market entirely."

"Not if I can track down the Maverick."

Nick straightened and stared at her, plainly stunned. "Track down the . . . the damn thing disappeared years ago. Even if you did find it, it's probably not for sale."

"But I can try, Nick. In fact, I've already done some preliminary research."

His expression closed off. "You didn't tell me that."

"Why should I? It's just a start. But Nick, I think we should go after it. I'm not the only one asking questions about the Maverick these days."

"What do you mean?"

"Everyone I talk to about it comments that mine is the second request they've received. Someone else wants it, too. If we move fast enough, maybe we can locate it first."

He dropped his head to the back of the chair and closed his eyes, weariness radiating from him. A tiredness she didn't understand. "Let it go. The Maverick is dead."

"But Nick, if we could get our hands on that design, maybe even locate the man who designed it —"

"It's dead, I tell you." Nick jumped from the chair and started pacing.

"What's wrong? What do you have against the Maverick? It doesn't make sense for you to say let it go. If I can find —"

He whirled around on her, fists clenched at

his sides, pain shooting from his eyes. *"I'm* the designer, damn it. The Maverick was mine, and it's gone, dead, just like the man who stole it from me. Dead and buried. Just leave it that way."

Sixteen

Sammi was stunned. "You? Why didn't you tell me?"

"Tell you what? What a fool I was? And how stupid a man can be?"

"Nick —"

"I was so hot to design that plane, so eager to see it roll off the production line, to fly the first one myself. Dad . . ." He shook his head. "You know how it's been between us. He told me I was crazy, so I went elsewhere."

"To Sam Barnett."

Nick snorted. "Yeah, good ol' Sam. Dad warned me not to trust him, but I wouldn't listen. In those days I didn't care about anything but getting the Maverick in the air."

"What happened?"

"I had my head buried so deep in designs and tests, I didn't pay any attention to what Barnett was doing. We had cut a verbal deal on the future profits, but I should have known better. He filed all the paperwork with the FAA and with his attorneys in *his* name. Then the son of a bitch went and got himself killed in a car wreck."

"And the rights to the design went to his heirs."

"You got it. His heirs. His son, to be precise. Bob, the recluse. The one none of the detectives I hired could ever find. I was left with no legal claim to the Maverick, and no way to get it."

"Oh, Nick. No wonder you never wanted to talk about the Maverick. But," she said, an idea coming to her, "if you did it once, you could do it again."

"Do what?" he asked tiredly.

"Design the jet."

For a split second the light of enthusiasm flared in his eyes. Then it was gone. "No. I couldn't do it. I put too much of myself into the Maverick to ever want to try again. Besides, I can't run Elliott Air if all my time is spent designing."

"All right." She conceded because she saw how much it hurt him to talk about the Maverick. "I'll let it go." *For now.* "But one thing I don't understand is why you went to New Orleans if you weren't interested in developing a business jet."

He turned his back and stared out the window, watching a King Air B200 take off from Wiley Post in the late-morning sun. "I had my reasons."

"Oh." And they were obviously none of her business.

"A couple of them, as a matter of fact," he said, surprising her. She had thought, from his tone, the subject was closed.

He paced back to the chair next to her and sat down. With his hands clasped, eyes downcast, he leaned forward and braced his elbows on his knees. "One was to see if anybody had heard anything on Bob."

"Bob?"

"Barnett. Sam's son. I . . . guess I was still hoping he would surface, and along with him, a chance to get the Maverick back. I should have known better."

Sammi kept quiet. He wasn't in the mood for more of her arguments just then. She would save them for later. She had no intention of letting the subject of a low-cost business jet die, but it could wait. Just then what she really wanted to do was run her hands through his thick, dark hair and smooth the lines from his brow.

A foolish notion.

"My other reason for going," Nick said, raising his gaze slowly to meet hers, "was you."

Sammi's breath locked in her throat. All she

could do was stare at him, wishing . . . wishing for everything at once. That she was far away in that moment so she wouldn't have to hear what he said. That he meant what she wanted him to mean. That they had never gone to New Orleans. That they were still there.

"We've talked business, Sammi. Now it's time to get personal."

Sammi stiffened. She couldn't deal with this, not from a man who lashed out at her and accused her of what he had accused her of. She didn't care if he meant it or not. He had said it. That was bad enough.

She couldn't deal with Nick on any personal level, she knew. She felt herself slipping under the spell of those deep blue eyes. How long would it be before he snapped his fingers and she jumped, before she stopped living her own life, thinking her own thoughts, and became merely an extension of him? Before she threw herself down on the floor to become his doormat.

How long before he tired of her?

With more calm than she knew she had, she said, "There is no us."

"There is," he said softly. "You know there is."

She closed her eyes. "No. There can't be."

"There can be," he said with force. "All you have to do is say yes."

She opened her eyes and looked at him. "Say yes to what? To carrying on some secret, sleazy affair during our lunch hours? Or would you rather I quit my job and become your full-time mistress?"

A muscle along his jaw twitched. "I'm not asking either of those things, and you know it. All I'm asking is for you to give us a chance, Sammi. We shared something special that last night in New Orleans. I'd like—"

Sammi could feel herself leaning toward him, wanting him, yearning for him. If she let him go on, no telling what she might agree to. So she interrupted him.

"You'd like everyone to keep talking about how I sleep with you to keep my job?"

Nick burst from the chair and braced his hands on the arms of hers, trapping her there. "Damn, but you're stubborn. What's important here?" he demanded. "What we can have together, or what other people might think?"

He pushed away and stood over her. "If you think I'll let this gossip go on . . . if you care more about what other people think than you do me, then forget it. I don't want to come *after* your job, *after* the opinions of every single person you ever met. I want to be first, damn it. I love you. I thought you felt the same. I thought that's what New Orleans was all about.

I guess I was wrong. You're just as stingy with your emotions as you are your money. I should have known."

Sammi gasped. "What's that supposed to mean?"

"It means," he said, his eyes growing fierce, his face hard, "that neither of them, love nor money, does you any good if all you do is hoard it. You'd rather take the chance of ending up stranded one day than turn loose of a few dollars for a new car. You'd rather deny what you feel for me than take a chance that we can make it work. You're a coward, Sammi."

Sammi couldn't face the pain, the fury, the censure in his eyes. She fled the office.

Sammi reached for another tissue and blew her nose. Again. The box of tissues was nearly empty, and no wonder. By three o'clock Saturday morning she had been crying on and off for a day and a half. And after all that time, she had yet to explain to herself exactly why she was crying.

"Because I've lost Nick," she whispered into the darkness.

You ran him off.

That voice again. Her own undeniable conscience.

She hadn't run Nick off, she had walked out

on him. What he asked of her, she didn't have
the strength to give.

What did he ask?

He wanted her to open herself up to the possibility of immeasurable pain. She couldn't do
it. Couldn't give herself to him, let herself love
him, then watch him walk away from her and
turn to another woman. She wouldn't be able to
bear it.

That's not what he asked.

No, she thought with a sad smile. Not really.
All he thought he was asking was for her to
love him. What he didn't realize was that she already did, and it terrified her. She had spent the
past three years of her life growing up, becoming an adult — finally — learning to think and act
for herself. If she let herself love him, would
she end up being just an extension of Nick, his
shadow, always standing in the background waiting for him to motion her forward when the
mood struck him?

Sammi sat up abruptly. Would she? Was it
possible for her to revert to that nonentity she
had been for so many years?

The answer came to her in a flash. No.

And if Nick loved her enough, he wouldn't
ask it of her, nor want it.

Another tear trickled down her cheek. He had
said he loved her, but the words, instead of being whispered tenderly or shouted with pride,

had come spewing from his mouth like molten rage.

And no wonder. He was baring his heart to her, asking her to love him, and what had she said? Good God. She had spouted some nonsense about what other people might think.

"Oh, Nick, I'm sorry."

She had tossed his love back in his face. She had hurt him, and badly.

Even before that scene in his office Thursday, she had denied his words. He had stood before her that morning and proclaimed that the night they made love had been the most incredible night of his life.

And then he accused her of sleeping with him to persuade him to build planes.

He explained that.

Yes, he had. But she had been so hurt, so angry over that damned rose, she had ignored him. She thought back to Thursday morning, trying to piece together what he had said.

It came to her slowly, like the sun breaking through heavy clouds one inch at a time. She remembered waking in his arms and the panic that had gripped her at the thought that one night would be all he wanted from her. She remembered his arms pulling her close and she could still see herself pulling away from those arms. She remembered his lips on hers and how she turned her head away.

She had hurt him! With all her insecurities firmly in place that morning after their incredible night together, with her fear that she wasn't woman enough for a man like Nick Elliott, she had pushed him aside and rushed to catch a plane. And every time he had tried to talk to her during the flight to Dallas, she had changed the subject. He had tried again at the Dallas airport. He had wanted to talk about their night together. But she had been too afraid he would tell her it couldn't happen again, when she already knew that, so she had interrupted him and asked him about building planes.

Good God. How could she have been so blind? So incredibly stupid? And so cruel as to let him think she cared about the opinions of others, when what she really worried about was the strength of her own backbone.

And a stupid worry, at that. For suddenly she understood just how strong she had become during the past three years. And she understood what Nick meant when he had compared her finances to her emotional state. He was absolutely right. For years she had been hoarding not only her money but her love, too. By using Jim's debts and his betrayal as an excuse to avoid spending money and by not admitting her love for Nick, she was still giving Jim control over her life. But no more. No more hoarding money or love.

She kicked off the covers.

It was time to spend a little of both. The first would be easy. The second ... Dear God, would Nick still have her?

And then another question—was she woman enough for him?

She clenched her fists. *Woman enough? Hell, yes, I'm woman enough. It's about time I proved it.*

At two o'clock Saturday afternoon, Sammi ignored the butterflies in her stomach and pounded on Nick's apartment door. The modern complex where he lived, with its tasteful landscaping of the terraced lawn leading down to the duck pond, was a far cry from her own apartment building. Sammi might never have found this place but for Henry's directions.

Not hearing a stirring inside, she pounded again. He had to be there. His car was in the parking lot.

After her third knock the knob turned and the door swung open. The expressions that crossed Nick's face made her ache. Surprise, a flash of hope, then wariness, distrust, before he managed to school his face into an emotionless mask.

She couldn't imagine what expressions crossed

her own face as she took in Nick's appearance. His dark cloud of hair looked like it had been combed repeatedly with his fingers and nothing else. Stubble shaded his jaws and chin, giving him a dark, dangerous look. Then there was his chest.

Her knees felt suddenly weak. It took considerable restraint not to fall against that bare expanse of muscle and dark hair, not to reach for it, run her hands over it until her palms tingled.

His only clothing was a low-riding pair of baggy gray sweatpants. So low . . .

She jerked her gaze back up to his face and took a deep breath. She had to concentrate, to do this right. "Hello, Nick."

He stared at her with those blank blue eyes for a long moment before asking, "What do you want?"

There was no hint of accusation in his tone, no recrimination, no censure. No emotion whatsoever. The very emptiness of his neutral voice made her eyes burn. She took another deep breath. "I have something to show you. May I come in?" Instead of waiting for an answer, Sammi stepped past him into the apartment that was a sharp contrast to hers.

Where her own was utilitarian, stark and bare of all but a few personal items, almost cold, Nick's apartment was a warm, personal home. Plush carpeting and overstuffed sofa and chairs in muted tones of brown and green made the perfect backdrop for what were obviously mementos from his world travels.

On the bottom shelf of the glass-topped coffee table a chunk of black lava leaned against a white piece of petrified coral the size of a football. The painting over the sofa was a pilot's view of the sky, clear and bright with a few eye-level clouds. She would bet her last dollar that most of the books lining the shelves on the far wall were about planes and flying.

"You wanted to show me something?"

"Yes," she said. "Off the balcony."

She crossed through the small dining room to the balcony doors. Yes, Henry's instructions had been perfect. "Right there." She pointed toward the east edge of the parking lot.

"The Corvette taking up two spaces?"

"Can't have that metallic-blue paint getting scratched. It's a 1980, complete with raised hood, ducktail spoiler, and mags." She turned slowly to face him. "I bought it this morning."

Light flickered across Nick's eyes, then disappeared, leaving them wary, cautious. At least they weren't blank any longer.

He folded his arms across his chest and leaned a shoulder against the glass door. "Is that what you came for, to show me your new car?"

"That." She swallowed. "And to tell you

something."

"Tell me what?"

Another swallow. Her palms were sweating, her heart was pounding. "That I love you."

Nick stiffened. Had he heard her right, or was he hearing his own wishful thinking? "What did you say?"

Her eyes turned dark. "I love you."

For one long eternity he hung there against the cold glass of the patio door, afraid to move, even to breathe, in case he broke the spell.

But this was no fairy tale. She was here, standing before him, saying she loved him. Her tear-filled eyes, her trembling lips told him she spoke from her heart.

"Sammi." He crushed her to his chest so hard he knew he must be hurting her, but he couldn't stop, couldn't let go. The way her hands gripped his back told him she wanted him to hold her tight. "I thought I'd lost you," he said between kisses. "I didn't think I'd ever hear you say those words."

She moved against him and almost set him on fire.

"Oh, Nick, I'm sorry I've been so stupid."

"Later," he said without taking his lips from hers. "Tell me later."

He had a thousand questions to ask, many things he wanted to say to her. But not now. Now was not the time for words. Now was the time to show her how much she meant to him. She was his world, his life. No woman had ever meant more to him than flying, but with Sammi, the thrill of flying paled to insignificance.

He swept her into his arms and kissed her face, her throat, every place he could reach, while he carried her to his rumpled bed. He swept the tangled covers aside and laid her on the sheet. With her arms tight around his neck, she pulled him down with her.

"Yes," she whispered.

"Yes," he answered. "Yes."

Clothes disappeared and bodies heated. Nick tried to slow down, to show her the love and care he would spend the rest of his life giving her. She wouldn't let him slow down. Her movements, her lips and tongue, those tiny whimpers from the back of her throat drove him to fevered heights. He plunged into her, burying himself body and soul in her sweet, hot depths.

"Yes," she cried. "I love you."

He wanted to answer, but couldn't. His heart was too full for words, his need for her too great.

Hearts pounded. Lips devoured. Flesh seared flesh. Two souls soared together. Then Sammi cried out his name and pulled him right over the edge of the world with her. With his final thrusts, the words broke from his heart, from his locked throat. "I love you."

It was the goose bumps that woke Nick up. They were caused by Sammi's slender fingers threading through his hair from his scalp to the ends. She let the hair fall, then started over, letting it drift through her fingers. Each touch of those fingers against his scalp and hair sent another delicious shiver down his spine. He smiled against her breast.

"You're awake."

The softness of her voice eased through him. He raised his head and met her smiling gaze. "Know what I want?"

She shifted her thigh and felt him spring to life. Her smile widened. "Yeah, I think I do."

Nick laughed and kissed the mole beside her mouth. Then he kissed her lips. He pulled back and sobered. "That's understood. But there's something else I want."

"What?"

Her throaty whisper nearly took his breath away. "I want to wake up like this every morning for the rest of my life, with you in my arms."

Her eyes widened, her lips parted.

"I love you, Sammi." His heart whacked against his ribs. "Will you marry me?"

Her eyes widened even more. He felt her

heart race to catch up with his.

"Nick . . ."

He waited. Could he have been wrong? Could she not feel what he felt? Did she not understand how special they were together, how strong their love could become? God, was she going to tell him no?

Her throat worked up, then down, but she didn't say anything.

"Sammi?"

"I . . ." She swallowed again. "I . . . I'll probably do stupid things without realizing it that might make you mad, and I love my job. You'll have to fire me to get me to quit. And I want you to promise you'll at least think about redesigning the Maverick—not for me, but for you, because it means so much to you. But—"

"Sammi—"

"But I love you so much that I can't imagine my life without you. Yes, if you'll have me, I'll marry you."

"It's about damn time. I was about to give up on the two of you."

Nick and Sammi looked at each other in wonder, then burst out laughing.

It was Sunday afternoon before either saw a stitch of clothing again. After a quick lunch they had decided it was time to tell Henry their plans. They had rushed to his house—in Sammi's Corvette—dying to tell him their news, and Henry wasn't even surprised.

Well, Sammi thought, if their impending marriage couldn't knock that smug look off his face, maybe she still had something that would.

"All right," she said, "try this one. If the—"

"When," Nick interjected.

"Right. When the Product Liability Bill passes Congress, the Skybird 2000 goes back into production."

"I expected that," Henry said calmly.

Sammi frowned at Nick. "Can we trade him in on a different model? This one thinks he knows everything."

Nick grinned. "Tell him the rest."

Sammi pursed her lips. "Nick has decided if he did it once, he can do it again. He's going to design a new version of the Maverick."

Henry's brows nearly touched his hairline. "Well, I'll be."

"Hah! We got him," Sammi cried.

"You're really going to do it?" Henry asked Nick.

Nick gave him a wry grin. "As soon as I figure out how to do that and run the company at the same time. You don't know of anyone who'd like to take over for me, do you?"

After a stunned moment Henry's eyes lit with

308

a twinkle. "Well, I might. I just might. Matter of fact, I'd do it myself, but I would put a condition on it."

"What condition?" Nick asked.

"That you don't start over on the Maverick."

Sammi watched Nick's elation disappear into dismay. Her own heart sank. She had nearly talked herself hoarse getting Nick to agree to design the new jet. Why was Henry against it?

Nick arched one brow. "If I don't design the plane, I won't need anyone to take over the company for me, will I?"

With a secret smile, Henry said, "Oh, I don't know about that." He lifted a thick manila envelope from the table next to the sofa and tossed it to Nick. "That ought to keep you out of the front office for a while."

Nick hefted the envelope in his hands. "What is it?"

"Open it and see. But you might want to sit down first."

With a wary eye on Henry, Nick sat on the sofa. Sammi leaned over his shoulder as he pulled out the contents.

The first words she spotted made her vision blur. "Nick!"

Nick's head jerked up. His mouth dropped open.

With misty eyes, Henry nodded. "It's exactly what you think it is, and it's in your name, as it should have been from the beginning."

Slowly, after a hard swallow, Nick looked back down at the papers in his hands. "The Maverick," he whispered reverently.

"But . . . how . . . ?" Sammi asked.

Henry sat down next to Nick. "The detective agency I hired finally tracked down Bob Barnett. Found him with his head shaved, selling flowers on a San Francisco street corner. He was only too happy to part with some of the "useless worldly goods"—his words, mind you—that his father left him. I would have told you sooner," he said to Nick, "but I wanted to wait until I had the documentation in my hands."

Nick finally tore his gaze from the papers and looked at Henry. "I don't understand. You were against this project from the beginning. Why go to all this trouble?"

"Because I was a pigheaded jerk. I should never have been against it. I ought to have backed you all the way. The Maverick should have been an Elliott aircraft from the first pencil drawings. This is my way of saying I'm sorry, of asking your forgiveness."

Sammi watched with stinging eyes as the two men, father and son no matter what anyone said, hugged each other.

"Are you going to bring those papers to

bed?" Sammi asked that night.

Nick hadn't been farther than two feet away from the documentation on the Maverick since Henry had handed it to him that afternoon. Nick looked up at her now and laughed. "Of course not." He tossed the papers onto the dresser and crossed to the bed. He leaned down and nuzzled her cheek.

"Are you sure?" she asked, teasing him.

"Why would I want a Maverick, when I can have you?"

Oh, what was he doing with his tongue? "You can fly a Maverick. You can't fly me."

Nick raised his head. The sheer heat in his eyes took her breath away. "Oh, yes," he whispered. "Yes I can. I'll show you."

And he did.

Epilogue

Dozens of floral arrangements decorated every available surface of the private room in Oklahoma City's Baptist Medical Center. The door eased open. Sammi smiled as a giant bouquet of red roses surrounded by baby's breath seemingly walked into the room on its own two legs.

Henry's face peered from behind the arrangement. "May I come in?"

"Please do," Sammi said. "There's someone here who wants to see you."

Nick squeezed Sammi's hand, then released her to take the bouquet from Henry.

Free of his burden, Henry edged toward the bed. "And how is the world's most perfect grandson?"

Just then David Henry Elliott kicked free of his light blanket and reached his arms up.

Nick, clearing a space for the flowers, laughed and shook his head. "Heaven help us, he's spoiled already."

"He's not spoiled," Henry said firmly. "He just wants his grandfather, that's all."

Henry traced a finger down the tiny leg.

Sammi sighed and closed her eyes. She was so grateful for everything in her life. For Nick, for their beautiful day-old son, for Henry.

She shuddered to think what her life would be like if she hadn't applied for that job on the assembly line at Elliott Air five years ago. The job had given her so much. She had regained her self-esteem and confidence, she had an exciting, challenging career, and good friends. But most of all, the job had led her to Nick.

She heard him approach the bed and opened her eyes. He raised her hand to his lips and kissed it. His eyes glowed with such love and devotion, a lump rose in her throat.

"Dad's right about one thing," Nick said. "David is perfect. And so," he said, leaning down to kiss her forehead, "are you."

"More perfect than you know," Henry said with a strained voice.

Sammi and Nick looked at him where he leaned over the baby still resting in the crook of Sammi's arm. Henry held one tiny foot in his hand, staring at it in awe.

"Henry?" Sammi asked, a tingling of premonition racing down her spine. "What is it?"

"Thank you, Sammi," Henry said fervently. He leaned down and kissed the baby's head, then Sammi's cheek. "You don't know what you've given me."

"The world's most perfect grandson?" she asked, worried about the look in his eyes.

"Yes, and he's *my* grandson."

"Of course he is," Nick said. "We settled that question a long time ago."

"No," Henry said. "I mean this child is my grandson, literally."

Sammi felt her heart race. A tense look came over Nick. "What do you mean?" he asked.

"Haven't you seen the mark on the sole of his foot?" Henry asked.

"It's just a birthmark," Sammi said.

"Yes." Henry grinned, his eyes filled with moisture. "I know it's a birthmark. I—" His voice broke. His gaze sought Nick's face. "I have one exactly like it. So did my grandfather."

Sammi smiled through her tears and watched her husband and father-in-law embrace at the foot of her bed. Lord, Lord, those blind stubborn fools. If they had only bothered to look at their own photo albums anytime during the past twenty years, they would have known what she knew instantly the first time she had seen a picture of Henry in his twenties.

The two men, at that age, had looked so much alike there was no mistaking their relationship. Not as far as Sammi had been concerned. She had tried to get them to see it once, but they had shied away.

315

They had decided they were comfortable with their relationship. The question of Nick's actual sire no longer troubled them, for they had agreed they were father and son in heart, if not in fact.

Sammi had let them get away with it, knowing there would come a time when they would both realize the truth, that Nick was Henry's son in every way.

That day had finally come. She shifted the slight weight of the baby against her arm. "Thank you, sweetheart," she told her son, "for doing what should have been done years ago."

This child would never have to doubt who his family was. His grandfather was Henry Elliott, a pioneer in the aerospace industry. His mother was Samantha Carmichael Elliott, a woman who knew her own mind, her own worth. His father was Nick Elliott, the man his mother loved with all her heart.

DISCOVER DEANA JAMES!

CAPTIVE ANGEL   (2524, $4.50/$5.50)
Abandoned, penniless, and suddenly responsible for the biggest
tobacco plantation in Colleton County, distraught Caroline Gil-
lard had no time to dissolve into tears. By day the willowy redhead labored to exhaustion beside her slaves . . . but each night
left her restless with longing for her wayward husband. She'd
make the sea captain regret his betrayal until he begged her to
take him back!

MASQUE OF SAPPHIRE   (2885, $4.50/$5.50)
Judith Talbot-Harrow left England with a heavy heart. She was
going to America to join a father she despised and a sister she
distrusted. She was certainly in no mood to put up with the insulting actions of the arrogant Yankee privateer who boarded her
ship, ransacked her things, then "apologized" with an indecent,
brazen kiss! She vowed that someday he'd pay dearly for the lib-
erties he had taken and the desires he had awakened.

SPEAK ONLY LOVE   (3439, $4.95/$5.95)
Long ago, the shock of her mother's death had robbed Vivian
Marleigh of the power of speech. Now she was being forced to
marry a bitter man with brandy on his breath. But she could not
say what was in her heart. It was up to the viscount to spark the
fires that would melt her icy reserve.

WILD TEXAS HEART   (3205, $4.95/$5.95)
Fan Breckenridge was terrified when the stranger found her near-
naked and shivering beneath the Texas stars. Unable to remember
who she was or what had happened, all she had in the world was
the deed to a patch of land that might yield oil . . . and the fierce
loving of this wildcatter who called himself Irons.

*Available wherever paperbacks are sold, or order direct from the
Publisher. Send cover price plus 50¢ per copy for mailing and
handling to Zebra Books, Dept. 3835, 475 Park Avenue South,
New York, N.Y. 10016. Residents of New York and Tennessee
must include sales tax. DO NOT SEND CASH. For a free Zebra/
Pinnacle catalog please write to the above address.*

CATCH A RISING STAR!

ROBIN ST. THOMAS

OFFICIAL ENTRY FORM
Please enter me in the

Lucky in Love

SWEEPSTAKES

Grand Prize choice: _____

Name: _____

Address: _____

City: _____ **State** _____ **Zip** _____

Store name: _____

Address: _____

City: _____ **State** _____ **Zip** _____

MAIL TO: LUCKY IN LOVE
P.O. Box 1022A
Grand Rapids, MN 55730-1022A

Sweepstakes ends: 2/26/93

OFFICIAL RULES
"LUCKY IN LOVE" SWEEPSTAKES